I0620774

KUMITE FOR LOVE

JUDY MALCOLM

For anyu and apu

CHAPTER 1

"*R*eady to go again, Peter?" Aiyana Amari said and took deep, re-energizing breaths.

Peter stroked a hand over his sweaty blond hair. His fair face was flushed and he pressed his lips in a straight line. Pained brown eyes stared at her from under arched brows. "We've been going for hours," he said. His voice bordered on whining.

"Come on, Pete. Don't get soft on me," she said and tightened her black belt.

Peter shook his head. "Aiyana, do you ever *really* listen to what you say?" He walked across the hardwood floor and drank from the fountain near the change rooms. At this late hour the few members who used the club were long gone.

Aiyana snorted and smoothed back a few wisps of hair that had fallen out of her ponytail. "Focus, Pete." She faced the mirrored wall and threw gloved punches through the air.

"Okay, okay. But don't go full-out. I don't feel like icing anything." Peter retrieved gloves from the floor and fastened them on. Aiyana practiced a few high kicks and then hopped on the balls of her feet.

"Get over here already. If you move any slower I'll miss my

flight." Her voice echoed through the gym—her safe haven. Her father had established it when she was just a baby. The dojo had been her playground. She grew up watching her dad, the great sensei, teach martial arts. Everything was perfect until that horrible day, almost eleven years ago.

They stood across from each other and popped in their mouth guards. She tried not to laugh at his pout. Cute looks aside, he was lean, ripped and a worthy opponent. They locked eyes and their previous banter was replaced with silent concentration. They bowed and after a ready, set, go, began their match.

Aiyana immediately took the offence. Consecutively, she punched Peter in the chest then delivered a side kick to his midsection. The fight ended in seconds.

"Yes!" Aiyana jumped in victory. "I'm ready for Japan, aren't I?"

Peter unfastened his gloves and tossed them back on the floor and spat out his mouth guard. "I've never seen anyone move as fast as you, Aiyana."

She punched him lightly on the shoulder. "Thanks, Pete." She turned, picked up a rope and started skipping.

"But, Aiyana, just because your offence is faster than most U.S. competitors doesn't mean it will be in Japan."

Aiyana stopped and dropped the rope. "What are you trying to do, Peter? Psyche me out?"

He winced. "Never. I just don't want you to be disappointed if you don't win. Aiyana, wait."

Not wanting to hear any more, she stomped into the change room. Her vision became clouded and she lost her balance. She shot her hands out and leaned on the vanity counter. Dehydration had probably set in, damn; she had been reckless by not having enough to drink. She took deep breaths and waited for the haze to clear. In the mirror she saw the vague outline of a dark-haired girl. Was she a champion or a dreamer? She pounded a fist on the laminate. No, stop. At this point there wasn't room for any doubt. She'd come too far and trained too hard.

The momentary dizziness dissipated. She reached down and grabbed her pre-packed knapsack and duffel bag from the floor and headed out through the deserted gym. She hadn't expected Peter to hang around. Her grumpiness over the past few weeks had finally driven him away.

Before exiting she paused and looked back.

I won't lose your gym, Dad.

She snapped off the lights and went outside. While standing under the large black and white AMARI'S DOJO sign, she locked the door.

"Aiyana."

She jumped. "Oh, Peter. You're still here?"

His shoulders slumped forward. "Yah. About what I said in there. I didn't say it to psyche you out or break your momentum or anything like that."

"I know, Pete. And you shouldn't be apologizing because you were right. I just have a lot going on in my head."

He nodded and leaned against the brick building. "Want a ride home?"

The dojo was located in a relatively busy part of downtown Akron and cars whooshed by steadily from both directions.

Aiyana shook her head. "I'm going straight to the airport."

"You already said bye to your mother?"

Tightness squeezed Aiyana's chest. "You could say that."

He leaned forward with his mouth slightly open and his eyes half closed. His minty, warm breath caressed her face. As his lips inched closer her body tensed and she turned her head. He stepped back and looked down. In the awkward moments that followed he plunged his hands into the pockets of his pants and jingled his keys.

"Peter, I'm so sorry. Call me stupid." She bit her bottom lip and wished she felt more than friendship for him.

He shifted his gaze from the concrete sidewalk to her eyes and forced a smile. "Hey, it's all right. You'd think I'd have gotten the message by now. Right? Well, have a great trip and knock 'em down. And don't worry about the place—I've got it covered."

She stepped forward but stopped herself from hugging him. "Thanks for being the truest friend anyone could have."

He nodded. "No problem. Good-bye, Aiyana."

"Bye, Peter."

He walked away and her eyes moistened. Why did this good-bye feel so final? She punched numbers into her cell phone and waited. Minutes later a taxi squealed to a stop and she got in to catch a red-eye flight to Tokyo.

CHAPTER 2

Soft brown curls surrounded her mother's ethereal face and dark semi-circles underlined her sad, azure eyes.

"You don't have to go for him...your father died in that same competition, what if something happens to you? Stop chasing dreams, Aiyana...there's more to life than martial arts..."

Aiyana startled awake and heard the steady hum of the plane's engines. She glanced at passengers around her and leaned back into her seat. The recent argument with her mother still stung, a lot. She took a deep breath and grabbed the booklet from the seat in front of her. *WELCOME TO JAPAN.* She flipped through pages listing restaurants, museums and historical facts. She read about a festival being celebrated the next day, July 7th, and then saw a whole page advertising the Meiji Tournament. Her heart fluttered. She slipped the booklet into her knapsack on the floor.

"May I get you a drink?"

Aiyana glanced up at the Japanese flight attendant. Her round face had flawlessly powdered skin, lined eyes, soft pink cheeks and lips. Her pinned up shiny black hair didn't have a strand out of place. Aiyana felt plainer than usual.

"Um, yes. Water please."

The woman gracefully handed Aiyana a plastic cup and bottle and pushed the cart forward. Aiyana checked her phone. She'd been cramped in her chair for a long sixteen hours and tried to stretch. When the wheels hit the runway at Tokyo International airport she breathed a sigh of relief.

After de-boarding, slipping through customs and exchanging dollars for yen, Aiyana stepped outside into thick humidity and beaming sun rays. She placed a hand over her brows and flagged a taxi. She opened the door and spoke in Japanese. "Can you please take me to the Temple Inn?"

The driver nodded. She tossed her bags in the back seat and climbed in. She looked out the window at the steady stream of cars and buses and studied everything she saw. Pagoda style architecture was interlaced with massive, modern buildings. Monochromatic crowds of people in blacks and grays scurried along sidewalks, and then Aiyana saw a burst of color of a geisha wearing an orange kimono with a yellow obi or sash. She gazed at the woman's small, graceful steps and the gown's wide sleeves and flowing fabric. The woman stood out like a colorful butterfly.

The taxi turned onto a road along a river where a multitude of cherry trees lined the bank. She imagined the branches filled with pink and white flowers and how breathtaking and fragrant the blossoms would have been a few months ago. Along the shore a young couple embraced, looking into each other's eyes. And then they kissed. A strange ache tugged inside Aiyana's chest and she looked away. Maybe she should have let Peter kiss her. She took the water bottle from her bag and drank the last gulp. She needed a good run.

The driver turned into a driveway flanked by massive willow trees, drove by an expanse of grass dotted with bonsai trees and then stopped at a pagoda building capped with a red clay roof.

She paid the driver and with her bag in hand she entered the spacious foyer of the Temple Inn. Scrolled pictures lined the walls and she marveled at the intricate lines of each drawing. She jingled the bell on the unoccupied reception desk and in moments a short, elderly man shuffled in.

"Can I help you?" he asked in Japanese.

She had no problem responding in his native language, her dad had taught her well. "I'm Aiyana Amari. I'd like to check in."

The man put on his glasses and flipped to a page in the ledger. "Yes. You have room two fourteen." He turned the book around for her to sign and placed a key on the counter. Behind thick lenses his eyes widened.

"Hoshikosan," he said in a whisper.

"Excuse me?"

He pointed to the portrait behind him. "Hoshikosan. You bear a strong resemblance to her. She was also known as the blue-eyed geisha."

Aiyana raised a curious brow. "Blue eyes?"

"She was a famous geisha. Rumors say Shogun Ieyoshi fell in love with her and died of a broken heart after she left."

Aiyana leaned forward to get a closer look. The sketch was drawn in shades of black and white, except for the eyes. The azure irises were captivating. Had he truly believed she looked like the woman in the picture?

Aiyana shook her head and felt oddly sad by the tragic story. "Other than the eyes, I don't see the resemblance. And I'm only half Japanese." She held up the key. "Thanks for this." The man bowed and she headed toward the dark wooden staircase, climbed the stairs and walked to the end of the hall. Inside the room she flicked on the light and kicked off her cross-trainers. Tatami mats covered the dark oak floor and rosy walls matched the floral bed comforter. She set the alarm clock on the night table then looked behind a partition in the corner of the room

7

and found a toilet and a sink. The view out the back window displayed a lush lawn and a bridge over a pond of koi.

Oh, Mom. Why couldn't you have come?

She pulled her cell phone from her knapsack, thought for a moment then put it down. No. She had nothing more to say to her mother. She dropped to the floor and did a series of sit-ups, crunches and then rolled onto her stomach for push-ups. When she was done she put her shoes back on, grabbed the key and her wallet and went for a jog.

She ran along the main road into a busier part of town and then slowed to a walk, gasping for breath. Even though it was evening the heat and humidity persisted and made exercise impossible. Most likely the long flight had also taken its toll. She passed by several stores and thought this would probably be the only chance she'd have to shop so she entered a souvenir boutique.

Inside, shiny kimonos in blues, reds and yellows were displayed on a circular rack. On the other side of the store were shelves of ceramics, rows of vases, bowls and teapots. There were also bins of plastic samurai swords, armor and nunchuks. Aiyana equated the items on display to those in a dollar store. In here Japanese culture had seemingly become commercialized and somehow it made her sad. Her stomach rumbled and she headed toward the door. She'd seen enough.

"May I help you find something?" A middle-aged sales lady in a calf-length black kimono walked over. "A souvenir? Perhaps a teapot for your mother?"

Aiyana froze for a few moments at the mention of her mother. "No, thank you. I was just leaving."

Before she could walk out the woman spoke again. "Excuse me, please, are you sure you want to leave so soon? There must be something you would like me to find for you."

"Well, if you really want to know," Aiyana glanced around, "I'd like to see anything more, authentic. Something with history and a story."

The woman smiled and raised an index finger. "I understand. You thirst for knowledge of the ancient ways. I can see an old soul in the light of your blue eyes. And your aura is bright red— you are very passionate, energetic, and competitive."

Aiyana's mouth had dropped open and she snapped it shut. Hairs rose at the back of her neck. How could this woman sense so much about her?

"Please, follow me, I have such items."

Intrigued, she followed the woman to the back of the store. They entered though an archway of hanging beads into a dark storage room. The woman pulled a string and turned on a ceiling bulb, barely brighter than a candle.

"You'll search in here?" the woman said.

Aiyana shrugged. "All right. Just a quick peek."

The sales woman walked out and Aiyana glanced around. Boxes of various sizes were stacked randomly about the room. A Samurai of old painting adorned one wall and a picture of Mount Fuji under moonlight adorned another. The cluttered shelf at the back of the room housed random articles and she went over to get a closer look. She rummaged through items and examined straw baskets and hand-carved wooden geta shoes. She found a fan and opened it slowly. The aged paper appeared brittle but still held firm and revealed an artful display of white cherry blossoms. Carefully she put the fan back on the shelf and decided she should be on her way. Suddenly the overhead light flickered and buzzed. Afraid the bulb threatened to burst; she stepped back and kicked her heel into something hard. She turned and saw an antique chest tucked in the corner of the room. The light stopped buzzing and shone brighter, illuminating the dragon figure carved on the lid. She crouched and ran her hand along the etched camphor wood surface. Compelled to see inside, she lifted the lid and drew in a quick breath. There on top luminesced the fabric of a silvery turquoise kimono. This fine silk was definitely genuine. She beheld the authenticity she had so craved to see. Who had worn this dress? And when? This kimono was fit for royalty.

Tucked in beside the kimono was an elegant black lacquered box. She picked it up and opened the lid to reveal a jumble of painted sticks, silk flowers, and ornamental combs—all decorative hair accessories. She tried to push the lid down but it wouldn't budge. It had locked open. Suddenly, and she didn't know how, the box flipped out of her hands and crashed to the floor, scattering its contents.

The sales woman rushed in and Aiyana scrambled to pick everything up. "I'm so sorry. I don't know how I did that."

The woman crouched. "It is fine. I will help you."

As Aiyana replaced the items she noticed something she hadn't seen earlier—a gold ornamental hair comb. Along its edge was a row of perfect pearls, marred only by a single empty center crevice. She picked it up and an electric shock sparked blue. "Ouch," she cried and dropped it into her other hand. She examined the lustrous element that in her opinion looked to be real gold. As she held it in her palm the cool metal warmed, many degrees in mere seconds, so much so that it felt like she had a chemical hand warmer in her hand. She didn't trust her senses. Her heart pounded harder as the heat radiated.

"You know," the woman said, oblivious to Aiyana's situation, "that once belonged to an exotic geisha, with blue eyes like yours. Stories say the emperor fell in love with her then died after she suddenly disappeared."

"A geisha? Really? It's lovely but hardly worth the price of slavery."

The woman giggled. "Geisha is no slave."

"Then what would you call it? I mean, it's certainly not a life of your own. You basically live to serve and please men while wearing the most uncomfortable clothes created, beautiful but uncomfortable."

"Have you ever worn kimono?"

Her wardrobe consisted of her gi, track pants and sweat tops so she shrugged her shoulders. "No, I haven't."

The woman smiled. "The geisha life is good. Yes, geisha entertain, but they have a rich life and have opportunities to influence important people."

Aiyana knew better than to continue this debate. Japanese culture was entirely different from American culture. She had read and studied much about it and could even understand and respect their philosophies. But the bottom line was that she was born and raised in the US and she didn't like women being restricted in any way from following their dreams.

Aiyana stood and smiled at the sales woman. "I do believe that the geisha life would be interesting, if that was the geisha's choice of course." Aiyana put the comb into the box and closed the lid, easily this time. She handed the lacquered box to the woman. Strange. "A minute ago that hinge wasn't working properly. Well, thank you for showing me this room. Now I don't have to visit a museum, even if I had the time."

"You not staying in Japan anymore?"

"Yes, I am. But I will be competing in the Meiji Kumite."

"That is an old tournament, and an honor to compete. It is traditional, like geisha life."

Aiyana laughed. The woman just drove a point home. "Yes, it is, and it is the reason I am here. I want to be part of it. It was nice meeting you."

Aiyana walked through the beaded archway and across the store. When she opened the door to leave the sales woman called out and caught up to her. "Here, you take this."

Aiyana looked down and saw the fancy gold comb in the woman's hand. "No, I'm sorry, but I can't afford that."

"This is a gift, so you remember authentic Japan." The woman folded the hair ornament into a sheet of white tissue paper and handed it to Aiyana.

Aiyana hadn't expected this act of kindness. She would accept the gift so as not to insult the woman. "Thank you very much. *Arigatoo.* I will be honored, if you come to watch the tournament."

The woman bowed. "No, it will be my honor."

CHAPTER 3

The sun had set by the time Aiyana returned to the Temple Inn. The reception desk stood empty and Aiyana couldn't resist inspecting the portrait of the blue-eyed geisha a little more closely. Maybe there was a slight resemblance between her and the lady in the portrait. None the less, the person in the drawing didn't look very happy. Aiyana's stomach growled and she turned and jogged up the stairs. Her hands shook as she unlocked the door. Once inside she flipped on the light, pulled her new gift from her pocket and dropped it on the bed. She went to her knapsack on the floor to grab a protein bar and then noticed a tray on the table.

Food. Buddha bless who ever had arranged this hospitality tray. She grabbed the chop sticks and shoveled heaping portions of sticky rice and smoked fish into her mouth. The green tea was still warm. When she finished eating and drinking she stripped down to her tank top and jockeys. She sat in the center of the bed and carefully opened the tissue-wrapped hair ornament. Light danced mystically on the golden comb. Its sheen mesmerized her and when she touched it the metal remained cool. She couldn't explain how it had heated up in the shop.

Maybe it hadn't and she had just imagined it. She went to the mirror and pulled the elastic out of her hair—long locks fell loosely around her face and shoulders. With the comb she smoothed back some hair and then secured it in. To get a better look, Aiyana turned sideways to see her profile. The slight movement brought on a tidal wave of dizziness. She sucked in a breath and tried to steady herself. This was her fault. Once again she had exerted herself too much and had fasted too long. Her electrolytes and blood sugar were most certainly out of whack.

Suddenly, the room spun wildly as if she was standing in the center of a tornado's vortex. She couldn't breathe, couldn't move or see anything around her. She gasped. She was being pulled down, lower and lower and was totally overtaken by enshrouding blackness.

Aiyana rolled onto her back and felt a breeze caress her face, neck and arms. She opened her eyes and noticed the ornamental comb on the floor beside her and remembered what had happened. Relieved to feel no traces of dizziness, she sat up. The rays from the rising sun filtered in. *Crap, the competition!* She scrambled on her hands and knees to look at the time on the clock radio. She opened her eyes wider. The clock radio was gone and so was her bed. Her heart pounded hard and she jumped up to turn on the light but couldn't find the switch. Behind the corner partition the toilet and sink had been replaced by a wooden tub. Her backpack and suitcase were gone as well. Where did everything go? Was she even in the same room?

Aiyana opened the door and a young girl in a gray kimono shuffled by, carrying a bucket of steaming water and a towel.

"Good morning," the girl said and put the towel on a stool and poured the water in the tub.

Aiyana followed her. "What happened to my room? And where are my things?"

The girl stood several inches shorter than Aiyana and was perhaps a little younger. Her hair was tied into a tidy knot at the base of her neck. Her petite, square face had perfect creamy skin with pink cheeks and full lips. Her onyx eyes looked at Aiyana with confusion. Maybe she had trouble understanding Aiyana's Japanese accent so Aiyana spoke slower.

"Where are my clothes, and my shoes, and my passport?"

The girl bowed. "If you so wish, I will fetch your kimono now."

Aiyana grimaced. "Kimono?" What was going on? Still clad only in her underwear, Aiyana picked up the towel and wrapped it around herself. She threw open the door and froze. It couldn't be. This was the same room at the end of the hallway. Something was wrong. Very wrong.

As Aiyana headed to the staircase she saw a woman wearing a deep red kimono and black wig shuffle into a room at the other end of the corridor. Aiyana cautiously descended the stairs and looked around with every step. This place was the same, but different.

When she got to the lobby there was no desk clerk because there was no desk. And no drawing of that blue-eyed geisha. Terror squeezed her throat. She sprinted out the front door and down to the road, a dirt road with no asphalt and no sidewalk. When she looked up she saw a rickshaw. The driver wore a pointed dome hat and ran while pulling a cart with two passengers. There were no automobiles, not a one. Down the road there were no towering buildings, just trees. Every passer-by wore either a kimono or loose shirts with calf-length trousers. No one wore jeans, tank tops or baseball caps.

There was no doubt that she was in Japan. The burning question was, in what century? In horror, Aiyana took a step back.

She must be dead.

CHAPTER 4

*A*iyana turned and ran across the front yard, into the lobby and up the stairs to her room. She paced on the woven mats. Was this Heaven or Hell? She thought she had only fainted last night but maybe she'd had a stroke or heart attack and had actually died. Or, more optimistically, maybe she was in a coma with her spirit floating in a historical world. If she was in a coma she'd have to wake up soon. She had a tournament to compete in.

An idea popped into her head and she pinched herself in the forearm, hard. It hurt. As far as she knew, dead and comatose people felt no pain. That left her with a final possibility. She had actually travelled back in time.

Aiyana crouched at the tub and splashed water on her face. Time travel. It couldn't be. She didn't believe in it yet here she was. She splashed more water when the young girl appeared beside her, holding a garment the color of a peach.

"What year is this?" Aiyana rushed her words.

The girl raised her brows. "It's 1853. Are you all right, Hoshikosan?"

"Hoshikosan? Is that what you think my name is?"

The girl nodded.

"And what is your name?"

"Mariko."

The door flung open and an older woman in a black kimono entered. Her hair was pulled back tightly into a bun and her wrinkled lips were the color of blood. She glared at Aiyana.

"You're not dressed yet? Your danna is waiting downstairs. Mariko, hurry." The woman clapped her hands and left.

Aiyana stared after her. "Who was that? And what's a danna?"

If the girl thought Aiyana had lost her mind her expression hadn't shown it. "That was Mother Yokomata. She is in charge of the geishas in this house." Mariko went over to the chair at the vanity. "Your danna is a gentleman who has paid for your company. Please sit, Hoshikosan."

Aiyana walked over and dropped into the chair, just like she had apparently dropped into the life of a geisha. She bit her lip. "And what exactly do I have to do in his company, Mariko?"

The girl casually arranged accessories in the table. "Nothing you haven't done before."

What did Mariko think she'd done before? Aiyana stiffened.

Mariko picked up a flat brush and dipped it in a round silver tin. The tip came out white.

"Oh, God, I'm going to be painted like a clown," Aiyana said quietly in English and closed her eyes. She couldn't fight her way out of this situation so she'd play along until she figured a means to get home.

Mariko dusted Aiyana's face with powder then lined her eyes and brows with a coal pencil. Lastly, with a fine brush Mariko painted Aiyana's lips. Mariko smoothed some kind of fragrant oil through Aiyana's hair and swiftly tied it into a loose knot. Mariko then reached for a black wig.

When Aiyana saw it she shook her head. "Sorry, Mariko. No wig please."

The girl bowed, backed away and picked up the kimono for

Aiyana. Aiyana stood and put her arms into the wide sleeves of the silky robe and then Mariko tied a white obi around Aiyana's waist. Next she pulled on white silky socks and slipped her feet in wooden geta clogs. Aiyana glanced at her reflection in the mirror and leaned closer. Was this really her? Her hair glistened and her skin resembled fine porcelain. Her lips were the color of a velvety red rose petal and her eyes appeared even bluer. The transition was astounding.

"Holy crap, Mariko. I'm the caterpillar that just morphed into a butterfly."

"Hoshikosan?" Mariko said. "What language did you just speak?"

Aiyana smiled. "That was English. I'm from America."

The girl's mouth slackened and she stared at Aiyana in wonder. "You truly are exotic."

Aiyana shook her head. *This could not be real.*

Mother stood in the doorway and gave a single nod of approval, despite the absence of the wig. "Hoshikosan, come." Aiyana looked at Mariko, shrugged, and then followed mother out the door. She nearly tripped from the confining kimono around her ankles and had to shorten her strides by half. She felt like a galloping pony in her geta clogs and on the hardwood floor she sounded like one too.

She took cautious steps as she followed 'Mother' down the stairs. What was she in for with her danna? If he became lecherous he'd regret it. They stopped at a paper-panel sliding door. Mother removed her shoes and knelt down. Aiyana hesitated then did the same. Once they were both kneeling Mother slid the door open. On their knees they shuffled across the threshold and closed the door behind them. Aiyana felt like she had a fish tail instead of legs as she stood.

Across the room she saw the broad back of a tall blond man. Not the danna she had expected to see. He wore a loose white shirt, snug black pants and shiny black boots. This guy looked like a Viking. Maybe he woke up in the wrong century too. In a swift motion he turned around.

Aiyana stared at his tanned, sculpted face. The top of his shirt was loosely laced and gaped open in a V, revealing fine blond chest hair and well-developed pecs. His dimpled smile drew air from her lungs.

He bowed. "My apologies for having had my back towards you, but everyone in this country moves around as quietly as ghosts. I am Captain Derek Blackburn."

Mother cleared her throat and introduced Aiyana as Hoshikosan. Aiyana become more self-aware and awkwardly curtsied. She cringed—she should have bowed. At least she hadn't shaken his hand or given him a fist pump. He hadn't seemed to notice her blunder.

Mother shuffled up to the captain and he handed her a pouch. She examined the contents carefully.

"I assure you, my lady, it's all there, plus a tip." He spoke in English.

Mother looked at the captain then at Aiyana. "What did he say?" Mother asked Aiyana.

"Oh." Aiyana realized Mother needed a translation. "He said he paid you extra because he likes your hair."

For the first time Aiyana saw Mother crack a smile, a closed mouth one, but a definite smile. She turned to Aiyana.

"Hoshikosan, the table is set for you to perform a tea ceremony for this kind foreigner." Mother bowed and backed out leaving Aiyana alone with the captain. Aiyana gulped as the captain stepped closer.

"You are even more beautiful than the last time I saw you, if that is indeed possible."

Aiyana shook her head. "It's not."

He raised his eyebrows.

"Captain, I just arrived here, so you see, it is not possible that you have seen me before, not that it isn't possible that I am more beautiful, which is of course always possible with make-up or surgery. Even if you have seen me before you wouldn't have recognized me. Trust me, normally I look totally different so I hate to say you are terribly mistaken." Aiyana took a deep breath.

He raised a brow. "I assure you, I never forget a face. Shall we begin?" he said.

"Ah, begin?" She hoped he wouldn't get out of line because knocking him out would be a bigger challenge than she had initially thought.

He gestured to the low black table on which sat a red teapot, two small cups, bowls and a whisk. On the floor, red cushions surrounded the table.

"Oh, yes," Aiyana said in relief. "Tea time."

She shuffled to the far side and dropped her knees onto a cushion. The captain sat cross-legged across from her.

"Are you comfortable?" she said, surprised at her hospitality.

"I am," he said in a strong, rich voice.

She tapped her fingernails on the table and averted his eyes. "Good. That's good." She found this situation too weird. As good-looking as he was, she wanted to get out of there. After making his tea she would resign her job.

As a child, Aiyana had often performed the tea ceremony for her father. He had always complemented her on her grace and said her hands did a magical dance. With this warm memory she confidently rearranged the dishes in front of her. Derek leaned forward as he watched.

"So you said this isn't your first time in Japan, Captain?"

"No, it's not."

"Well, it's my first time."

The captain raised his eyebrows but didn't question what she said.

Aiyana poured some boiling water into a bowl and added a

spoonful of powdered bright green tea called matcha. She whisked the mixture until it frothed then poured it into the teapot.

"Captain, did you know the tea ceremony is based on the Buddhist belief that there is beauty in even the simplest things." She poured two cups of tea and placed one in front of him. Only then did she notice he was staring at her face instead of his beverage.

"That is a lovely belief, encouraging people to appreciate what they have." He picked up the cup. It looked small in his hands. He took a sip and licked his lips. "This is good. Sweet without sugar." He put the cup down. "Now, Hoshikosan, did you say you just arrived?"

So he had decided to call her out on what she had said. "Yes."

The captain laughed. "You speak fluent Japanese, make tea like a native and you say you just arrived? And besides, my dear woman, the only ship in the harbor is mine."

"But I didn't arrive in a ship." Her voice trailed off when she realized what she said and decided to change the topic. "Tell me, Captain, where are you from?" He rested his elbows on the table and looked at her with intense hazel eyes.

"Originally from America, but for the past few years I've been sailing for the Dutch."

"Why do you sail with the Dutch and not the Americans?"

"Japan doesn't allow American ships to enter. Only the Dutch and a few other select countries are allowed to trade goods."

Aiyana sipped her tea. "So you are here to trade?"

He looked at her more closely. "Partly. I'm discovering that Edo is a beautiful city—the geisha even more so."

Aiyana's cheeks grew hot and she was glad he didn't seem to notice as he continued his story.

"But, it's the samurai and shogun I have a problem with. Barbarians, the whole lot of them."

"You know, Captain, it won't be long before Americans, as

well as the whole world, will be able to trade here. And the samurai, well, they won't have a good fate."

"Inconceivable. How could you presume to know such things?"

Aiyana laughed. "Inconceivable? You haven't heard anything yet."

The captain narrowed his eyes. "What haven't I heard?"

Aiyana took a drink of her tea and placed the cup down. "All right. I'll level with you. You seem like a cool guy. Just try to keep an open mind."

"Level?"

"Yes, that means I'll tell you something. Lay my cards on the table."

He nodded. "You are a woman who plays cards?"

"Yes, but not now." She took a deep breath. "I'll try to explain this even though I don't really understand it myself. I came to Tokyo to compete in a martial arts tournament."

"Tokyo?" he said, appearing confused.

"Yes, exactly. Edo is called Tokyo in the twenty-first century. Somehow I was transported back in time. I'm originally from Akron, Ohio. I'm not a real geisha, I'm a kumite competitor."

He burst out laughing. "Not a geisha you say? Everything suggests otherwise."

She didn't know why but Aiyana felt she had to convince him. "Listen, Captain. Last night I was in my room upstairs, in the twenty-first century. It was late, I was getting ready for bed, then I put an ornamental comb in my hair. Suddenly the room started spinning and I couldn't see and I blacked out. When I woke up, here I was, in 1853."

"Enough! What I see is that you are speaking of something impossible. Perhaps you should just accept your fate and fulfill your obligation to me."

She drew in a slow breath before speaking. "Don't you understand? I never agreed to any obligation." Thoughts raced through her mind. "The comb. It's the link. Once I pin it back in my hair I'll be transported home and be able to compete. That must be the way to leave here."

He clenched his jaw. "You wish to leave Edo?"

"Yes, more than anything and now I figured out how." Aiyana rocked back on her heels and stood. With a swooshing sound, she quickly shuffled across the room, out the sliding door and up the stairs to her room.

Aiyana looked around and found the ornamental comb on the vanity table. The gold seemed to possess a permanent sparkle. She picked it up and heard footsteps. In the mirror Aiyana saw the captain's reflection. He towered over her, his shoulders twice as wide as hers. Her heart skipped when their eyes met. Slowly Aiyana turned toward him.

"See, Captain, this is it." With him only inches away she could almost feel the heat of him. His gaze was magnetic. He was magnetic. Once she put the comb in her hair she'd never see him again. Impulsively she gave in to the magnetism and moved closer. She lifted her arms to his shoulders, solid and muscular as she expected. She arched up onto her tiptoes and touched her lips to his in a farewell kiss. His lips were tender and his breath was warm. He hesitated for a moment then pressed closer, first with his mouth, then his whole body. Their lips parted and allowed their tongues to explore a suspended passionate kiss.

His arms pulled her closer; his whole body was strong and unyielding. Butterflies swarmed in her stomach then fluttered to her extremities. The heat of desire ignited within her and she pushed herself back. She breathed heavily. This felt real. Too real. Green flecks ignited in his hazel eyes and his breathing was as ragged as hers.

"My lady, I suppose I should apologize but I'm not sorry for kissing you. But, truth be told, you kissed me first."

Aiyana nodded. She had never kissed a stranger like that before, or anyone like that before. And now it left her wanting more. "You're right, Captain. I did move in first."

He looked down at her hand.

"May I see that?" he asked huskily.

"Of course." She held out her palm and he gently took the comb. He examined the back of it and then the front and brushed his finger along the empty crevice. "This is truly lovely and certainly one of a kind." His pupils were large and she couldn't help but wonder if he was talking about the comb.

"You say you will be leaving with this?" he asked.

She nodded. "It's the portal. I can't leave without it."

His fingers curled into his palm until the ornament was almost out of sight. Without warning he turned and walked to the door.

"Wait." Aiyana skittered after him. "May I have my comb back please?"

"No." His face had turned dark.

"No? Why the hell not?" What he had done was as sobering as ice water. He had completely washed out their romantic interlude.

"Now that I've found you I'm not permitting you to leave."

Her pulse sped. "Look, buddy, that's mine." She tried to pry his fingers open. "Give it to me." His fingers wouldn't budge.

"I'll return it when I'm ready. Let's say this is an added assurance that you won't be going anywhere." He started walking away.

"No, Captain. Stop!"

He stopped and waited until she shuffled up to him. He looked at her with smoky hazel eyes and her heart skipped again. "I have to go to my ship but I'll be back to share tonight's meal with you." He bowed, turned and left.

What a brute. How dare he steal her comb? Especially when

24

he knew how much it meant to her. Obviously he didn't give two figs about how she felt. Well, she would show him. He wasn't messing with an everyday geisha. She was a kick-ass girl from the future.

Oh why had she kissed him?

CHAPTER 5

*C*onfined by both her kimono and her predicament, Aiyana looked out her bedroom window at kneeling gardeners, hand trimming the grass. This was only one step up from watching it grow and she wanted to scream in boredom and frustration. It'd been hours since Captain Blackburn had snatched away her comb in his solid fist. She had made the mistake of trusting him and cursed herself for acting on the impulse to touch her lips to his. The kiss was pleasant and exciting, but certainly not worth the delay in getting home.

She needed to run and train, at the very least hit something. As she looked at the level, green yard she got an idea. It had taken all afternoon but she finally formulated a plan. A simple yet brilliant one. As soon as the captain arrived for dinner she would put it into action, quite literally.

There was a light rap on the door and Mariko entered carrying a kimono the color of a pink carnation. She bowed. "I will help you change for dinner, Hoshikosan?"

"Yes, please and thank you," Aiyana said and envisioned her scheme yet another time. While being distracted by her thoughts she allowed Mariko to dress her like a doll. Tonight, Aiyana would go through the dinner ritual, butter up the captain, and then pose her challenge. He seemed to be the type to not back away from a dare. Mariko finished by wrapping a wide yellow obi around Aiyana's waist. She hated the limitation and constriction of her clothes but in the end, a pretty flower attracted the biggest bumble bee.

"It is time," Mariko said. With dainty steps, they headed down the stairs. Aiyana broke into a sweat—not from exertion but from nerves. She bit her bottom lip and hoped her plan would work. They stopped outside the reception room and Mariko slid the door open for Aiyana. Aiyana took a deep breath and entered the room, forgetting to kneel and shuffle over the threshold.

Aiyana heard the door close behind her as she stood in front of the captain. This time he was facing her with his hands behind his back. He wore the same black boots but had changed into brown, form-fitting pants and a loose black shirt. He looked even bigger than before, if that was at all possible. Her pulse raced wildly, no matter how hard she willed it to slow down. His lips parted and his gaze roamed over her. She froze under the scrutiny.

"You are a vision, Hoshikosan," he said.

A flush crept across her cheeks. "So are you, Captain," she said and remembered to bow.

"Please, call me Derek. Shall we sit?"

"Yes, please, Derek," she said. How could her strong legs become this wobbly? Aiyana and Derek assumed their places on the cushions. On the table daisies were displayed in a pottery vase, chopsticks alongside various sizes of bowls.

Aiyana looked across the table. Right now his eyes were more brown than green, his lips were taut and he had a slight furrow in his brow. His expression was serious, as if contemplating something. His intense gaze, as well as the knowledge that not so long ago she had boldly planted a kiss on his full, perfect lips, made her feel uncomfortable. Remembering made her want to crawl under the table but that wasn't feasible. This moment felt too awkward and she wasn't sure how to put her plan in action. He still stared at her and didn't seem very compliant as of yet. Getting him to agree to her plan might possibly be more difficult than she had initially thought.

"Hoshikosan, why did you kiss me?"

Now she knew what he had been contemplating. The kiss. As far as she knew, women of this era rarely made the first move. Ironically, Aiyana had never made the first move even in her own era. She squirmed on her cushion. He had asked a good question, but what would she answer?

The door slid open and Mariko entered, carrying a bamboo tray. Aiyana let out a breath, relieved at the girl's perfect timing. From the tray Mariko transferred a deep saucepan and a wooden ladle to the table, and then bowed and backed away.

Aiyana stretched forward to look into the pot, picked up the ladle and stirred the broth. Creamy white tofu chunks, carrot slivers and green onion slices swirled around. Aiyana served a scoop into each of their bowls. There were no spoons so she picked up her chopsticks. For her, using chopsticks was as easy as using a fork. She put the upper chopstick between her thumb and first two fingers and held the other chopstick steady at the base of her thumb. She picked up a piece of tofu and slurped it in her mouth. She glanced at Derek. His dimpled smile showed his mood had lightened. She realized her folly and put down the sticks.

"Oh, I'm sorry. I think I should have let you eat first."

"No, please continue. I've never seen a geisha who looked like she actually enjoyed her food. Besides, I'm still learning the customs around here."

"Well, you seem quite accustomed to the hiring of a geisha." As soon as the words slipped out of her mouth she regretted saying them. Her plan wouldn't work if she annoyed him with snide comments. Thankfully he didn't look mad.

"It may seem that way, but, I have never wanted the company of a geisha, until now. You, Hoshikosan, are my first."

"I'm honored." She almost succeeded in speaking without a sarcastic lilt. "Please try the Miso soup, it's delicious." She couldn't wait to see his large hands fumble with the chopsticks. She almost giggled at the thought of him snapping them. To her surprise, he picked them up and handled them perfectly. He picked out chunks of tofu with the precise dexterity of a surgeon but eyed her more than his food. She watched his sensual lips move as he chewed and found it difficult not to be enchanted by his earthy eyes.

"Hoshikosan, I see you are in a better disposition than you were earlier."

"Yes I am, thank you for noticing."

"I'm glad."

"But, Captain…"

"Derek."

"Derek, you have to admit that it was wrong of you to steal from me."

He shrugged. "I only did what was necessary." He ate another bite.

"Necessary?" She forced out a breath and tried to keep her tone calm. "You had no right."

"But I do have the right. I paid quite handsomely for your company so I was only ensuring you uphold your commitment."

"That is where you are mistaken. I agreed to no such arrangement."

"All the more reason I need assurance you will stay."

Mentally she told herself to calm down and think straight. She should have left this topic well enough alone. This conversation wasn't getting them anywhere, except annoyed, and she needed him in good spirits for her plan to work. She put down her chopsticks and took a steady breath in and out to recompose herself.

"So, Derek, did you finish the business on your ship this afternoon?"

He raised his brows. "I did." He also put down his chopsticks and then picked up his bowl and drank the broth.

Aiyana left her broth where it was and noticed Mariko had entered again. She served entre foods, a pitcher of sake and two small cups. Aiyana forced down a smile and immediately filled a cup to the rim with rice wine.

"Here's a drink for you, Captain. And doesn't the food look wonderful. There's rice, pickled radish and chunks of tuna and squid. Eat up and drink up." She pushed the cup closer to him.

"Please, help yourself," he said.

Aiyana picked up her chopsticks and reached for a chunk of fish. The soft savory morsel dissolved in her mouth. "Wow, this beats a protein bar any day," she said.

He crooked a questioning brow but instead of asking what a protein bar was he reached for his sake. He downed it like a shot and she quickly refilled his cup.

"I was wondering, Derek, what specific business brings you to Japan? What do you trade?"

"Currently, we're shipping cotton and wool in exchange for Japanese pottery, art and silk."

Yes! He drank a second cup. Aiyana refilled it. "And are the trading profits worth it? I mean, sailing was so dangerous in the nineteenth century. There were pirates and huge storms that swallowed up ships."

"You're speaking in the past tense." Derek cracked a smile. "All right, I'll play along for a moment. Is sailing not dangerous in the future? Are there no storms, waves or cut throat pirates?"

Aiyana thought for a moment, hopeful he may be starting to believe her. "Of course there are still storms and waves, but the ships are better, bigger, more sophisticated. As for pirates, unfortunately they still exist. Scumbags."

"Scumbags?" Derek laughed. "Such titillating vocabulary." He finished his third cup of sake. "Back to answer your question. I sail for more than just monetary gain."

Curious, Aiyana hesitated before pouring the last dribbles from the pitcher into Derek's cup. "Really? What are the other reasons you sail? What could be worth risking your life for?"

Now his eyes seemed to be drinking her up. "An exotic geisha with a silver tongue, for one."

His deep gaze distracted her. He was the one drinking and she was the one losing mental awareness. "Derek, I believe you are the one with the silver tongue. Unfortunately, how would you risk your life for me when you won't even return such a small item of mine? I believe you have just given me empty flattery."

Derek chuckled. "Touché."

She smiled. He appeared to be in a good mood—her plan was moving along well. When Mariko brought in fruit for dessert Aiyana requested more sake. Now it was time to stroke his ego.

"Derek, I bet you are an excellent sea captain."

He put his hands behind his back and leaned on them. His chest muscles flexed, the chest that had touched hers not so long ago.

"Excellent you say?" He smiled. "Well, I haven't sunk a ship yet."

"And your crew, they must fear you, I mean, you being so strong and tall."

He nodded. "My crew knows better than to start with me."

Aiyana leaned forward. "Captain, I would like to pose a challenge to you."

"A challenge? What kind of challenge?"

"I would like to challenge you to a fight."

This time he tilted his head back in laughter. "I would never raise my hand to a woman, let alone a treasure like you."

Aiyana crooked a brow. "Is the strong and brave Captain Blackburn afraid of losing?"

"You speak nonsense," he said in a dismissive tone.

"Just hear me out. We could have a match, a sparring match, a kumite. Not a duel to the death or anything like that."

Derek wrinkled his brow so she continued to explain. "A kumite, you know, taps to the head or mid-section. Each hit to these zones are one point. Three points and you win. And, if you ground your opponent you automatically win because then they are at your total mercy."

"What would I win?"

"Me. And my co-operation."

"But I already have you, so to speak."

Aiyana exhaled. He was confident, which could work in her favor. If he didn't take this seriously maybe he wouldn't give much effort.

"You have me but you really don't *have* me."

Derek raised his eyebrows. "Continue."

"You see, right now I may leave when you aren't looking, comb or no comb." That was a bold-faced lie. "But if you win, I will promise to stay and be your companion and or translator, and not give you a hard time about it."

"I want more."

She swallowed. "More? What more?"

"Love," he said in all seriousness.

Aiyana's throat went dry. He wasn't wasting any time. "That is asking a bit much, isn't it? I mean, you can't make someone love you."

"No, but you can act like you do. And perhaps offer another kiss?"

Her cheeks grew hot. "I suppose so. But you can't force me to do anything I don't want to do." She didn't know why she added this clause since she had no intention of losing and upholding these promises.

"I would not do anything you do not desire. Now, if by a miracle you win, what do you want? Your comb?"

"Exactly." Damn. He probably figured out how much it meant

to her so this challenge could be futile—he may suspect that she wouldn't leave regardless. He was about to speak. Hopefully he missed her slip-up.

"Let me see if I understand correctly. If you win the kumite, I have to return your comb. If I win, you will give me your loving attention. And a kiss."

"Yes."

"Then I accept the challenge. Let's get on with this, kumite for love."

CHAPTER 6

*A*iyana arranged to meet Captain Blackburn in the garden. But first she went up to her room to shed her kimono and socks. With no available exercise gear she had to improvise. Her camisole would serve as a tank top and for shorts, she pulled the back of her underskirt forward between her legs and tucked it into the front of her waistband. The getup looked ridiculous, certainly racy for this time period but necessary for the win.

She looked out the window and saw Derek facing the bridge and koi pond with his back to her. Even from a distance he looked huge and she would try to use his size against him. On the whole, women carried their weight and center of gravity lower than men allowing them to have better balance. She hoped this fact was true in the captain's case. Suddenly Derek turned and looked up. He noticed her staring at him and gave her a lazy smile. She sucked in her breath and quickly moved to the side of the window and pressed her back against the wall. Heat rose to her cheeks. Damn he affected her. She checked to make sure her skirt was still securely tucked into her waistband and with a leather strap she tied her hair into a ponytail. She pulled on a kimono and tied the sash like she would a bath robe.

It was time.

In bare feet she padded downstairs and out to the lantern illuminated garden. The immediate patch of grass was soft and velvety—the captain would appreciate this when he was flat on his back. Further out rounded fir shrubs dotted the lawn and the land gradually sloped and led to the domed bridge and trickling pond. The fruity, gently erotic scent of honeysuckle permeated the warm air. Such a beautiful setting, perfect for romance, even better for a sparring match that would gain Aiyana her freedom. She hoped no one saw them flitting about. The last thing she needed was for the captain to be thrown in prison or worse beheaded for raising a hand to woman.

Derek watched her approach and as she walked toward him she untied her sash, opened her robe and let it slip off her shoulders to the ground. His mouth dropped open. "Aren't you a sight to behold? I'm beginning to enjoy this outlandish request," he said as his eyes trailed over her.

"I know I'm a sight but this is necessary."

"Necessary, why? To distract me?"

She fought a giggle. "Derek, a kimono hardly allows freedom of motion." She looked at his feet. "You have to take off your boots."

"Is that a rule of the kumite?"

"Yes." She smiled.

Derek went over to a bench at the periphery and sat down. While removing his boots his eyes fixated on her bare legs. Heat rose to her cheeks and she felt exposed. He unlaced his shirt and pulled it over his head and dropped it onto his boots. Aiyana swallowed and tried to act casually after watching his striptease, though she couldn't stop sneaking glances at his thick chest and rippled abdomen.

"You know, you didn't have to take off your shirt," she said.

"I prefer it this way."

"Suit yourself." Now who was distracting whom?

They faced each other in the center of the yard with a distance of two arm-lengths between them. She squared herself directly in front of him, her eyes in line with his pectorals. She glanced up and saw the same lazy smile he wore earlier.

"Are we going to begin, Hoshikosan?"

"Yes!" She didn't mean to yell but she didn't want him to think she planned on staring at him all day. "First we bow to each other, but always keep your eyes on your opponent's." As they bowed she inwardly cringed because moments before she hadn't practiced what she preached when her eyes roamed freely over his body. "Now we are ready to begin." Aiyana bent her knees and held up her fists. This fight was of utmost importance. This was no preliminary round. This round meant elimination. She had to win to go home.

She took a deep breath. "Ready, set, go!"

Light on her toes, Aiyana started maneuvering around Derek, vying for a good position from which to strike. He held his fists up and looked like he didn't know what to make of her. He didn't bounce around, instead he moved warily. He waited for her to make the first move and she wouldn't disappoint him.

In the blink of an eye she swooped in for a double punch to his chest and quickly moved back again. She had to admit that she had punched harder than she normally would, but he could take it.

"That, Captain, was one point."

"Try that again," he said with a grin.

Of course she wouldn't do the same move twice. They circled each other for another revolution and then Aiyana threw a side-kick to his chest. The force of it knocked him back a few steps. Now he knew she meant business.

"Two, zero," she said in a loud bubbly tone.

"I see how much you want your freedom." His grin vanished.

Last round. Now she was getting excited. The first two rounds he hadn't seen her coming and hadn't reacted. She was slim and swift and just as she had suspected, his bulk had slowed him down. She could already taste her victory and she smiled— risky without a mouth guard. This time she wasn't taking any chances. She'd go in for a punch to the chest then a roundhouse kick. She had planned two consecutive maneuvers, just in case she missed one of them for some unpredictable reason.

Once again they circled each other. Then again, and again. She was as confident as a coiled rattlesnake about to strike unsuspecting prey. Her fist flew in for the punch but this time Derek reacted in a flash and ducked out of the way. She immediately shifted into her second maneuver and jumped. Just as she was about to kick him square in the chest he shot out a hand, grabbed her ankle and flipped her over. She landed with a thud, flat on her back. The wind was knocked from her and she gasped. She looked up at the sky and watched clouds float away, taking her freedom with them.

He knelt down on one knee. She saw what looked to be concern on his face. "Are you hurt?"

"I'm fine." She managed to choke the words out but didn't move. He didn't look convinced.

"Are you certain you aren't injured?"

She pulled air into her lungs. "Yeah, don't sweat it." Physically she'd be all right, but he'd severely bruised her confidence. Her world-class skills weren't good enough to best this captain, and her plan had failed miserably. She had over-estimated her skills and under-estimated his. He was the captain of a ship over 150 years ago so of course he could fight.

"Let me help you up." He reached out a hand but she ignored it and stayed down. He narrowed his eyes. "Now, what did you say I get for my victory? A kiss? And you will act, affectionately?"

She winced and rolled over to face away from him.

"Yes, Captain, that's what you've won."

CHAPTER 7

*D*erek stood over Aiyana and put out his hand to help her up.

"I can get up myself, I mean, thank you, Captain." She forced herself to take his hand. Despite being defeated she raised her chin. Once she was on her feet she pulled her hand out of his grasp and averted her gaze as she stepped around him to head back to her room.

"You will be leaving here in the morning."

Aiyana froze and then turned around. "I'm leaving?"

He picked up his shirt and put it on. "Naturally. You will be living with me during my stay in Edo."

She couldn't take this nightmare anymore, anger rushed through her veins. She turned and before running to her room she jumped into a roundhouse kick and hoofed a lantern clear off a pole. Once inside she dropped to her knees as tears of frustration streamed out. Normally she didn't indulge in self-pity but she couldn't help herself. Live with him? She thought she would just visit on occasion. She figured she could handle a couple of hours a day with him until she came up with another strategy to get home. But, all day, every day was an entirely different matter.

All at once her plans were shattered. She had agreed to a bargain she never anticipated to uphold but now had to.

She wiped away the last of her tears and Mother entered the room. Great. Now to top everything off, Mother would yell at her, or punish her by making her kneel on rice or something. If only her real mother was here.

"Hoshikosan," she said, though not as sternly as Aiyana had expected. "Mariko will be going with you to live with the captain. Your belongings are packed." She paused in the doorway. "You show too much emotion for a geisha. Remember, you are the one truly in control. Geisha can inspire men to do almost anything." Then she turned and walked out.

"Sure, the only problem is that I'm not a geisha."

Within these foreign walls Aiyana was filled with uncertainty and didn't want to admit to being frightened. After a whole day of scheming and anticipation her plan had failed horribly. Her body ached from the fight and when she tried to think, her mind refused to string thoughts together. The one thing she knew was that she wouldn't give up. There had to be another way to leave here and she'd find it. Like after a vigorous work-out, she needed to rest and refuel. Surprisingly, Aiyana slept well that night.

The next day Mariko entered and looked at Aiyana's state of undress. She held up a floral kimono for Aiyana to slip on.

"The rickshaw is waiting," Mariko said in her non-intrusive voice.

"Okay, let's get this show on the road." Aiyana glanced at Mariko as she got dressed. Mariko wore a wide-eyed puzzled expression. "Sorry, Mariko. Ignore what I said, the meaning was lost in translation." The girl's expression relaxed and together they headed down the stairs. Once outside she saw a man holding the handles of a hooded rickshaw. Mariko urged her to go ahead; Aiyana hesitated but then stepped up and in.

The rickshaw runner pulled them down the path to the road. From a distance, Aiyana took one last look at the Temple Inn.

They passed many people going about their everyday lives, carrying baskets and sacks. Other rickshaws also rushed along the roadway.

During their lengthy ride several rickshaw drivers switched off from pulling—their rickshaw was like the baton in a long distance relay race. When they finally stopped Aiyana's backside couldn't be more grateful to get off the hard seat. She and Mariko headed down a carved-out path through woods before entering a clearing with a wooden cabin and front deck. Aiyana looked out over the forest ridge at a three-masted tall ship anchored in Edo Bay's sparkling sapphire water. The captain's ship. The view inspired serenity—just what she needed.

"The captain has a lovely house," Mariko said. A couple of previously delivered trunks sat on the porch. "I will carry these in and unpack your things."

"I'll help, Mariko."

The girl slackened her mouth. "You don't have to, Hoshikosan."

Aiyana smiled. "I want to."

Mariko gave her a hint of a smile. They walked up two steps onto the deck and Derek appeared in the doorway. "Hello, ladies, welcome." He reached down and easily picked up a trunk. "Would you like to see where you'll be living?"

"Do I have a choice?" Aiyana asked.

"Of course you have a choice, Hoshikosan, and I believe you have already made it."

"That's right, I did." And he had to remind her. Aiyana squeezed past him and entered the house. Sheltered by trees, the cabin was cool inside with a pleasant cross breeze. Trace odors of smoke and incense filtered through the air. Mariko bowed and went to the pantry area to start preparing food. Derek brought in the trunks as Aiyana looked around.

The main front room was spacious. The floors were covered with tatami mats except for the center of the room where there was a square sunken ash pit. Scrolls of various sizes hung on the walls, enriching the room with scenes of farm fields, mountains and the one that really piqued her interest was the sketch of a sumo wrestling match.

"You like that one?" Derek said, standing behind her.

Aiyana nodded. "Yes, I do."

"Come, I'll show you where we sleep." He led her through a hallway to the back rooms. "Ours is the bigger bedroom." The first thing Aiyana noticed was the panoramic window with a view of the forest. At one side of the room was a table with two chairs. On the other side sat a hefty chest, the two trunks Derek had brought in, a futon mattress with several large white pillows and a thick comforter.

"Is that your bed or mine?" Aiyana said.

"Seeing there is only one bed it looks like we'll have to share." The corner of his mouth turned up.

"What?" She had never slept with a man before, let alone one she had just met. "I don't think so." She turned to walk out but he stepped in front of her.

"Hoshikosan, must I remind you of the bargain we made?"

"Not as long as you keep your end of it," she said in an even tone and hoped he noticed the defiance in her eyes.

"I suggest you rest now. I have work to do on my ship but later you will accompany me to a festival." With that said, he was gone.

She remembered reading about a festival on July 7th in the airplane flyer. She also knew July 8th was a significant day in history but couldn't recall what it was at the moment—so many other things circled her mind. She looked at the bed but rest was out of the question. There was too much adrenaline pumping through her. She untied her obi and began peeling off her kimono. Mariko entered the room and rushed over to help.

"You want to change clothes, Hoshikosan?"

"Yes, please. Let's take a look and see if they sent anything more comfortable." Mariko and Aiyana kneeled at the first trunk. A neatly folded white kimono patterned with pink hibiscus flowers sat on top. Beneath was another robe, burgundy patterned with yellow lilies. The other chest also had layers of kimonos, and then Aiyana noticed a black velvet bag. The bag was heavy and its contents jingled. She opened the drawstring and looked inside.

"Mariko, are all these gold coins mine?"

"Everything in there is yours."

Aiyana got an idea. "Mariko, can you do me a…" She paused to think of the word in Japanese. Then she remembered. "A favor?"

Mariko nodded slowly.

"Great. Can you go buy me some pants and shirts, like what the rickshaw man was wearing? And a pair of those flat black shoes? Can you do that?"

"Yes, Hoshikosan."

"Thank you, Mariko, I could kiss you." Aiyana handed Mariko a coin piece, then another, then the whole bag. "Here, take whatever money you need."

Aiyana escorted Mariko outside and squinted from the brightness as she watched Mariko disappear down the path. Once Aiyana got her new clothes and shoes she'd finally be able to exercise and run.

The sun shone like a laser, hot and bright and cicadas belted out their long, distinctive call. Aiyana decided to explore outside. She put on her clogs and went out in her underclothes. She entered under the canopy of trees and breathed in strong earthy scents. As she headed downhill she ducked under branches and snagged a leaf as she passed by. As she split the leaf into two she tried to formulate another plan. She thought of Mother's stern face and words of wisdom. *'You are the one truly in control. Geisha can inspire men to do anything.'*

Control? No. Captain Blackburn was definitely the one in

control. As for inspiring men, well, that was something she had never done, except for maybe encouraging Peter to kick higher while sparring. Perhaps this was the time to change that. She needed to pose another challenge to the captain. And the next one would be out of the ring. Her first plan had almost worked and she had to make sure that her second one was foolproof. She would have to get to know Derek better and find out what he wanted.

Aiyana stepped into a clearing and realized she'd walked all the way to the beach. Waves gently lapped the shoreline and the shallow water sparkled a transparent blue. The beaming sun overheated her in seconds and made the water look even more inviting. She looked out at Derek's magnificent ship, anchored a few hundred yards away. What she'd give to get a closer look. Men worked on deck but she didn't recognize anyone of them to be the captain. Sweat beaded her brow and she moved closer to the water. She glanced at the ship again—the men aboard hadn't seemed to notice her on this isolated shore. She slipped off her shoes and pulled the pins out of her hair, letting her hair fall around her shoulders.

She stepped into the cool water of the ebbing and flowing sea and waded in further until the rocky bottom dropped away. She tread water then dove under. The water enveloped her and she felt as free as a dolphin released from a theme park. Rejuvenated, she splashed around. Aiyana floated on her back and looked up at the wisps of clouds in the pale blue sky. Waves gently rocked her and she took a deep breath of the sea air.

Shouts of men disturbed her tranquility. She tread water and faced the ship. Several men on deck stood at the railing, hooting and hollering. Aiyana took a deep breath, plunged under and swam toward shore. She crouched in the shallows for several minutes. When she got out she ran as quickly as she could to the closest patch of greenery. She hunched behind shrubs, dripping wet with her thin cotton underclothes plastered to her. The next problem was that her shoes were on the beach. With the impending competition, she couldn't risk getting abrasions or an infection on her feet. She needed her shoes. Her thighs had become shaky and sore from squatting for so long but she had to wait until all activity on deck settled down. When the men moved from the railing and all seemed quiet, Aiyana ran to the shore. She picked up her shoes and risked another glance at the ship. A rowboat was being lowered with the captain sitting in it.

"Crap!"

Aiyana hurried up the hill and back to the cabin. The last thing she wanted was for a sailor after a long voyage to see her in a wet T-shirt. Especially when that sailor was Derek.

CHAPTER 8

*T*he sun was lower in the sky when Aiyana stormed into the cabin. She hunched over to catch her breath and saw Mariko crouching by the fire pit, stirring the contents of a pot.

"Oh, hi Mariko, you're back from shopping?"

The girl looked at Aiyana's wet underclothes but didn't ask questions or comment. "Yes. I'll show you the items I purchased for you—there are several," Mariko said.

"Unfortunately that'll have to wait. Mariko, can you help me get dressed quickly? The captain will be here any minute and we're going to a festival."

They hurried into the bedroom. Aiyana shed her wet clothes and pulled on a thin under robe. She sat in a chair while Mariko combed and pinned Aiyana's hair into a neat roll. Mariko brushed pale foundation cream on Aiyana's face and throat but left the highly erotic nape of the neck unpainted in the shape of a W. The naked skin alludes to other intimate parts men long to discover. With the burnt end of a blown-out match, Mariko traced Aiyana's lash and brow line. Lastly, Aiyana's lips were painted red.

Mariko retrieved a kimono for Aiyana to put on. When Aiyana saw it she drew in a breath. The pattern in the silk looked like peacock feathers in vivid blue, green and turquoise. "It's beautiful, Mariko, but I don't remember seeing it in the trunks."

Mariko shook her head. "It wasn't. The captain bought it for you."

Aiyana put her arms through wide sleeves and Mariko busily tied the kimono, then the blue obi. The fabric was meticulously crafted and the sewing and dying of the fabric showed intense labor. "Oh, my. This must have been expensive, Mariko."

The girl nodded. "That is for certain."

Aiyana looked forward in an unfocused gaze. She had never gone to prom or even had a date. She never knew what it felt like to receive a corsage or a gift from a guy, until now. Sure their circumstances were out of the ordinary, but it came down to the fact that Derek didn't have to buy Aiyana a gift. He chose to. And the thought of this gave Aiyana a warm feeling inside.

They heard a bang from the front of the house.

Aiyana widened her eyes. "Oh, no. He's home." She took Mariko's hands. "Thank you so much for helping me, Mariko. What would I do without you?"

For the first time, Mariko displayed lovely teeth in a wide smile. "You would do fine, Hoshikosan." She bowed and left the room.

Aiyana smoothed her hand along the front of her dress once more and glanced at the doorway. Derek leaned against the frame wearing a pleated shirt, black pants and boots. They locked eyes and his lips parted slightly, but not into a smile. His gaze made her heart pound harder and reminded her that she still owed him a kiss.

"You are a feast for my eyes," he said.

"So are you," she quickly reciprocated.

He smiled at her response. "Do you fancy the kimono?"

She stepped forward. "Derek, I don't know what to say. It's exquisite."

"I'm glad you like it. Are you ready to go?"

"I believe so." Aiyana slipped on her shoes. The captain offered her an arm and she accepted. She walked with tiny steps through the house and waved bye to Mariko. In an unhurried pace they strolled along the path to the road where a horse and carriage awaited. The steep step into the carriage presented a challenge. Aiyana contemplated hiking up her kimono when suddenly strong hands were on her waist. Derek easily lifted her into the carriage then took his place beside her. He picked up the reins and flicked them. With a start, the horse moved forward, its hooves trotted quietly on the dirt road. The sun sat low in the sky behind a range of trees.

"Did you have a pleasant afternoon?" Derek said.

Aiyana remembered floating in the ocean. "Yes, I did, thank you." She glanced at him and a corner of his mouth turned up.

"And how did you pass your time?"

Was he smirking at her? Had he seen her in the bay?

"Did you rest?" He probed further.

"Yes I did. For the whole afternoon." She answered quickly, perhaps too quickly.

"Then you are, refreshed?" he said.

She groaned inwardly. She was busted. He must have seen her frolicking in the waves.

Their wagon rolled into town and they passed by other buggies, rickshaws and pedestrians. Some men were accompanied by other geisha.

They turned onto a long wooden bridge. Aiyana looked at the water below and the high moat wall as the horse clip-clopped across. They passed through the large door of the Ottoman gate and entered the vast green grounds. The gabled rectangular palace had upwardly curved roof edges—a simple but gorgeous structure, set in quiet woods and surrounded by several watch-towers. They turned toward the vast park grounds where a crowd gathered and merriments were underway.

Derek pulled back on the reins and hopped off the wagon. Aiyana put her hands on Derek's shoulders as he lifted her down. His hands lingered on her waist and she dared to look up at him. For a moment she saw honesty in his eyes and time stood still. It wasn't the past or the present, just their time.

He slowly released her and turned to tether the horse to a tree. When he rejoined her he offered his arm once again. Together they merged with the crowd and headed to the center of festivities.

The captain seemed mindful of her limited mobility and kept his pace slow. She appreciated that. Looking around she was curious about something. "Captain, I'm surprised that you wanted to come here tonight. I mean, you don't appear to be the festival-going type."

He grinned. "And what type do you think I am?"

"The business, all-work type."

"Perhaps you are right, Hoshikosan. But then again, look where we are, at a festival."

Lanterns and colorful streamers lined the castle walls and hung suspended around the courtyard. Long bamboo poles were decorated with sheets of paper bearing notes. Samisen music filled the air and several young girls danced in front of them. The crowd grew by the minute. The captain pulled her closer—a subtle gesture, but Aiyana noticed it.

"Come, Hoshikosan, there is someone I want you to see."

Derek led her to a large tent on which hung purple velvet banners embroidered with emblems of the imperial coat of arms. Open front panels revealed ornate chairs inside, around which men in loose black robes stood. At the perimeter of the tent, several rotund men, probably sumo wrestlers, stood guard.

Derek leaned closer to her ear. "See that small, older man who is speaking?"

"The one in the gray kimono who just took a drink?"

"That's the one. He is the shogun of the Tokugawa clan," Derek said.

Aiyana squinted to get a better look. "Wow, he's one of the last shoguns."

"What do you mean?"

"Well, if this is really 1853, the shogun rule won't last much longer."

"Then who will rule? Emperors?"

"Exactly. In 1858, Emperor Meiji will govern, if I remember the history correctly. The tournament I'm competing in is named after him."

Derek frowned. "Such a thing is impossible for you to know."

"Not impossible if you're from the future."

Derek shook his head. "Hoshikosan, I pray you do not speak of such nonsense again. Travel to another time is impossible. Now, shall we get some refreshments?"

Aiyana slipped her arm out of his. Yes, time travel sounded impossible, she didn't blame him for his views. Up until a short time ago she felt the same way. But she wished he could at least acknowledge that she thought it was real.

"Are you thirsty?" he asked again.

Aiyana nodded.

Derek bought them cherry drinks and in silence they strolled from the crowd. They sat on a bench carved out of a massive tree trunk. Aiyana watched the last sliver of sun disappear beneath the clouded pink horizon. A breeze caressed her face and she watched the dancing lantern lights. This evening felt surreal, perhaps because, it was.

Aiyana sipped her drink. This place in time was captivating, intriguing and distracting. But she had to stop allowing it to disrupt her focus. She had to find a way to get home but as of yet she had no plan. She had to learn more about this man beside her then maybe a course of action would present itself.

"Derek?"

"Yes?"

His eyes glistened in the lamp light. His mouth looked relaxed, sensual. She straightened her back. *Focus.* "I'm curious. I know you had said you came to Japan to trade, but I see that since you have a cabin you are also somewhat of a resident."

"Yes, I suppose I am."

"I can't help but wonder if you have another agenda. Some other secret plan."

Derek slowly pushed up the sleeve of her kimono and exposed the bare skin of her arm. He stroked it with his fingertips, sending shivers over her whole body. Did he have a clue how this affected her? Probably not. Geisha were no strangers to the company of men and their touch. And to him she was a geisha, not an inexperienced girl.

"Hoshikosan, you are very inquisitive and I'll answer what you ask, though I am not sure how interested you will be in this matter."

"Try me."

He continued to stroke her arm as he spoke. She wished he would stop but a small fiber in her was glad he didn't.

"I began my career as an American sailor, though not a captain yet. There were three magnificent ships in our fleet. Miraculously, we had survived a perilous journey through storm after storm and by the time we reached the Far East, we desperately needed to make repairs, refuel and replenish our food and water provisions. The first ship that anchored was the unlucky one." Derek stopped touching her and winced.

Aiyana saw the painful memory in his eyes. "Derek, what happened?"

"The sailors that went ashore were slaughtered."

"That's horrible."

"It was. And the reason why I now sail with the Dutch. It's one of the few countries allowed to trade here."

Aiyana nodded. "Yes, the isolation policy." She knew Japan had closed itself off from the world for two hundred years.

Derek finished his drink and Aiyana did the same. He looked sad and probably preferred something more potent than fruit juice.

"You are well rehearsed in your knowledge of politics and social events. It is no wonder I had to pay so handsomely for your company."

His comment sobered her like a splash of cold water.

"So, Captain, that bag of gold was from you, wasn't it?"

"Yes."

"Do you want it back?"

"No. Not for all the world."

She swallowed hard. It was worth a try to get out of this unsigned contract. Still curious and wanting her questions answered, she inquired further. "Why did you come back here after witnessing such barbarianism? Aren't you afraid it will happen to your ship?"

"Cautious, but not afraid. I know some Japanese people don't welcome Dutch visitors either, but most are accepting and kind." He turned his head to look at her. "My secret plan, as you call it, is to persuade the shogun to open the country to foreign ships."

"Now that is one serious task. What did the shogun say?"

"I haven't had the opportunity to speak directly with him as of yet."

"Tough security, huh?"

"I beg your pardon?"

"Nothing."

He reached for her hand and held it. She had no idea if this was what a danna did with his geisha, but since Derek wasn't exactly a traditional danna she guessed it would remain a mystery, among so many other things.

He looked up into the dark sky. "Amazing, isn't it? Those are the same stars and moon I see no matter what part of the world I sail. This is an appropriate night for the Tanabata Festival. Wouldn't you agree?"

"I actually don't know anything about this festival—I hadn't come across it in my readings. Do you know what the Tanabata Festival celebrates?"

His lips formed a smile. "Actually, yes I do."

"Really? How?"

"This isn't my first time in Japan and I have picked up some of the language. I find that by pretending to not know the language I have an advantage."

"You'd hear what others were saying about you. Clever." Aiyana thought back to when she had translated for him, not so accurately, to Mother. Maybe he hadn't noticed. Aiyana looked up at the twinkling sky. "So, Derek, what is this festival about?"

"It celebrates two stars; the Weaver Princess and the Shepherd. They fell in love but neglected their heavenly duties, so the gods separated them by way of the Milky Way. Each year, on this one and only night are they allowed to meet."

"That is such a sad story—almost hopeless. What is one day out of a year? Not much."

"But, what would the year be without the excitement and anticipation of that one day?"

She nodded. "That's true, but it's still a sad story." Suddenly a plan unexpectedly presented itself the second she remembered the monumental event in history that occurred on July 8th 1853. "Derek, I believe I have a way to get the shogun's attention. Hurry!"

Aiyana and Derek meandered through the crowd. When they arrived at the shogun's tent Aiyana asked a guard for permission to enter but was denied.

Derek leaned closer to her. "I wouldn't waste my time. He won't talk to a civilian. You'll get more of a response from a tree."

In the tent the shogun stood among a group of men with his back to her. Then by pure luck he turned. Now was her chance.

Aiyana frantically waved her arms. "Come on, look over here." Still he didn't notice her.

"It's dark and they're too far away," Derek said.

She grimaced. "Captain, do you want to meet the shogun or not?"

"You know I do."

"Then stay a little more positive."

"Positive you say?"

"Yes."

"All right then. I am positive that the shogun is now leaving."

"What?" Aiyana looked into the tent. The men were bowing and began dispersing. Bodyguards surrounded the shogun as they escorted him through the courtyard.

Impulsively, Aiyana put her thumb and middle finger into her mouth and blew the loudest whistle she could muster. The group of men stopped and Aiyana waved and beckoned them over. The shogun's chief councilor and a bodyguard headed their way.

"What is your plan, Hoshikosan?" Derek said as he watched the approaching men.

"You'll see."

When the councilor came closer Aiyana noticed his exceptionally high forehead and a scanty mustache consisting of only a few long hairs. She would act and speak as formally as she could. She bent her arms and hid her thumbs under the long sleeves of her kimono.

"Good evening. My name is Hoshikosan. I would like to request permission to speak with the shogun."

"That is impossible."

"Please, it is very important. And it won't take long."

The man lifted his hand to silence her.

Damn him and his arrogance. "I have secret information he'll want to know."

He put his hand down but kept his nose up. "You may relay it to me," he said, wearing a sour frown.

"That won't be necessary." A voice said from the center of a group of guards. Shogun Ieyoshi stepped forward. "You may tell me directly."

Aiyana's jaw dropped and her heart thumped hard. She was about to speak with a real shogun. Derek pressed close beside her and she felt his body tighten. She bowed to the shogun. "Shogun Ieyoshi, thank you. I am honored. This is Captain Derek Blackburn, who sails for the Dutch and my name is Hoshikosan."

He nodded. Deep wrinkles creased his forehead and around his eyes. "Continue, Hoshikosan," he said.

"Thank you," she bowed again. "I want you to know that tomorrow, July 8th, 1853, four black ships will arrive from America, led by Captain Commodore Matthew Perry. He will offer you a treaty, requesting you open Japan to the rest of the world."

"That would be inconceivable, Hoshikosan. My scouts have reported nothing about this." The shogun stepped back and body guards swarmed around him. The chief councilor raised his snobbish brows at Aiyana then turned and walked away like a solemn bride with his long robe trailing.

They all thought she was nuts. And there was that word again —inconceivable. Well, they'd see about that, tomorrow.

CHAPTER 9

*A*iyana wanted to scream. Another plan of hers had fallen through. Derek still stood close but she felt his body loosen. She turned to look up at him. He seemed amused.

"Perhaps you should have fought him instead," Derek said.

"That's it," Aiyana said. "I'm out of here." She yanked up her kimono and ran into the crowd as fireworks exploded and crackled in the sky. She ricocheted into people like a pinball. She didn't care; it just felt good to run. For someone who confronted her problems head-on she sure was doing the opposite right now. She heard the captain calling out through the murmuring crowd after her, but damn it, her name wasn't Hoshikosan. Then she heard a bellow right behind her.

"Hoshikosan, I beg of you, stop!"

Aiyana knew this escape was futile. She halted but didn't turn and the captain leapt in front of her.

"Hoshikosan, don't ever do that again." His chest heaved with deep breaths.

She fought back tears though some escaped. "My name is Aiyana!" Booming fireworks resonated and bright exploding lights set the night sky ablaze. Her insides were just as volatile.

He put his hands on her shoulders, firmly but not hurting. "Just know that if you ever leave I will not rest until I find you. Understand?"

"Loud and clear."

With her mood for celebration gone, they departed from the festivities and walked in silence to the horse and wagon. She pulled up her skirt and stomped inside. Away from the crowd and the lantern light, only the captain was around to witness her un-geisha-like gesture. He sat next to her and flicked the reins. On route she could feel his eyes on her so she finally turned toward him. "What?"

"Does something not please you?"

"Yes. You have something of mine. May I have it back?"

"No."

"And you ask me what displeases me?" She had snapped at him and now feelings of guilt gnawed at her. She had made a bargain with him and she certainly wasn't upholding her part of it. They had a kumite for love, and she was acting rebelliously, not lovingly. And to his credit, after this last episode he hadn't reminded her of it.

"Captain, I owe you an apology. I haven't behaved as I had promised."

He chuckled. "I hadn't expected you to."

"Come again?" It was dark but she could still see the soft smile on his face and some tension left her body. "Then why did you make the wager?"

"I wanted to see where the kumite would lead. Now, I see you have your pride and I have no intention of humbling you. I was never good at breaking horses."

"Thank you, Captain, for comparing me to a horse." Aiyana smiled. She knew what he really meant.

He grinned back at her. "Furthermore, when someone shows that they love me it will be because they do, not because they lost a wager."

Rendered almost speechless, Aiyana felt a whole new respect for the man next to her. "Well, that's the way it should work."

The buggy turned toward a wooded area so she knew they were getting close to the cabin.

"But a final word of caution, Hoshikosan. I meant what I said earlier. You are not to leave me because it will be a wasted effort."

She didn't doubt what he had just said. And the thought of him impassioned enough to track her down sent a tingle through her. No one had ever pursued her that way before. He spoke and snapped her out of her thoughts.

"I have a question."

"What's that, Captain?"

"How do you know that American ships are coming? And how do you know Commodore Matthew Perry's name?"

"Well, Captain, I am who I say I am, so you see, events that are happening here and now I have already studied in history class."

"But who told you about the ships? Another officer? My crew have been sworn to secrecy. When I find out who he is he will be reprimanded."

He hadn't believed a single word she had said, but that was no surprise. Frankly she couldn't blame him. And while trying to understand his point of view her frustration began to dissipate.

"Captain, why is it a secret that the American ships are coming?"

"Naturally to not give the Japanese any warning and time to come to arms."

Well, she blew that secret by telling the shogun about the ships. But then again, the shogun and his arduous little advisor obviously hadn't believed her. She just wished she could see the amazement on their faces tomorrow when the Americans arrived.

"Derek, you knew the ships were coming?"

"Yes. But with sea travel one is never certain of exactly when. It would be ideal if I was able to assist in the negotiations."

The captain pulled back on the reins and the horse came to a halt. Aiyana moved to get off but this time Derek lifted her down, effortlessly. She stood in his embrace and her body sparked with desire. Her feet wouldn't move, but neither did his. His lips parted and a shiver ran through her. He slowly slid his hands away from her hips.

"You go inside," he said softly. "I'll finish up out here."

She walked a few yards then turned around, still a little unsteady after his embrace.

"By the way, Captain, for your information, the Americans are going to fail. So there will be no negotiations. Not this year anyway. Goodnight."

Aiyana went straight inside and didn't wait for any comment or reaction from Derek about what she had just said. Tomorrow when the ships arrived, Derek would certainly call it a lucky guess. This situation was frustrating and getting the best of her at times. She did propose a ridiculous notion. If someone came up to her and said they were from another century she would ask what narcotic they were on. But this was her, and she wasn't on drugs and she'd never make up such a story. There was no honor in that.

Unexpectedly, she thought of another plan and wrung her hands while thinking about it. It had to work because time was running out. She needed to present it to Derek tonight.

Mariko appeared out of nowhere as usual. She untied Aiyana's obi and helped her slip out of the kimono. Aiyana stayed in her underclothes and sat on a chair while Mariko unpinned her hair and then brushed it.

"There, all finished," Mariko said and smiled. "I have something for you, Hoshikosan."

Aiyana smiled turned to face Mariko. "The clothes?"

"Yes, and the shoes." Mariko pulled the items from a basket.

"You're an angel." Aiyana squealed as she picked up the silky shirts and pants. They looked like pajamas but she didn't care.

Now she could move, train, run and bring some normalcy into her life.

Mariko bowed and wore a serious expression once again. "Goodnight, Hoshikosan."

"Goodnight," Aiyana said and watched Mariko walk out. Aiyana carefully folded her new clothes and put them in one of her trunks. The single lantern on the table cast a pale yellow glow. Aiyana looked at the bed. She crossed her arms over her chest and moved to the other side of the room. She looked down at the captain's imposing sea chest. Not hearing any sign of his entry yet, Aiyana crouched to take a quick peek inside. There was no lock so she pushed open the heavy lid. Light barely reached this side of the room so she went to get the lantern and put it on the floor beside her. She looked through layers of folded shirts, pants, belts. Then deeper down, her fingers curled around smooth cold metal. She moved the clothes aside and realized she had just found a gun. Behind her she heard rustling. She looked over her shoulder and saw Derek approaching. She scrambled to quickly shut the lid and accidentally kicked over the lantern.

"Careful!" Derek hollered louder than an air horn. He lunged like lightning to grab the lamp before the kerosene and flame engulfed the straw mat and wooden floor.

Aiyana's hand flew to her mouth. Her heart beat wildly at the thought of almost torching the cabin. On a less serious note, she was also embarrassed Derek had caught her snooping through his stuff. Thank goodness he had moved so fast. He put the lantern back on the table and faced her. She was sure she wore a look of terror.

"I'm sorry," she said and sat on the edge of the bed. She realized she was shaking.

He sighed and dropped down beside her. He put his arm around her and she sagged against him. "I'm the one who is sorry, sorry for scaring you with my loud voice."

She smiled. "Well don't be. I was a klutz and you saved the day."

"I have seen the devastation of fires in Japan. Homes made of wood, straw and paper ignite like dry kindling."

"I'll be more careful next time."

He stood up and she glanced at him. He untied the string on his shirt and pulled it over his head. His tanned muscular body glowed like glazed bronze. He pulled off his boots and started to unbuckle his belt. Aiyana quickly looked at the floor. She wasn't ready for this. He walked over to her and she stared at his feet. Slowly she scanned up his legs to his shorts. She let out a breath of relief.

"I must look very different from what you are used to seeing."

He insinuated she'd seen a lot of not-so-muscular naked Japanese men. She dropped her jaw and snorted. Her bravado kicked in. "Actually, Captain, you are exactly what I like looking at."

He laughed. "Then I hope you won't be disappointed."

"Nope," she said with less confidence.

"Are you going to lie down?"

"Huh?"

"What side do you want?"

"Oh, this side I guess." She turned and tucked her feet under the sheet and then pulled it up to her chin. The captain extinguished the lantern and she watched his shadowy frame get into bed beside her. Frozen, she widened her eyes to see better in the dark. He moved beside her then became still. It didn't look like he was going to try anything so she let out the breath she was holding. He lay on his back with his hands behind his head.

After the previous distractions of a possible fire or the presentation of a full monty, now was Aiyana's chance to pose another challenge.

"Captain, are you sleeping?"

"Not yet."

"I know you don't believe how I know that the American ships will be arriving tomorrow." He didn't say anything so she continued. "I was wondering if you would be interested in making a bet."

Derek rolled on his side and faced her. "Another wager?"

"Yes. I'd like to bet you that Commodore Perry will arrive tomorrow. If I win, you will return my comb."

"And if I win?"

"But you won't."

"Then I won't make the wager."

Aiyana knew it was ridiculous for him to agree to such a bet and she felt like a child asking for the whole candy store. She asked for everything and offered nothing. She needed something to sweeten the pot.

"Okay, Derek, you're right. Let's see, how about if I win I get the comb and if you win…"

"I get my kiss."

Aiyana thought that sounded more than reasonable, especially since she knew she would win, providing all the history books were correct.

"Fine. That's fair. I will stop putting it off and give you the kiss I owe you."

"Now."

"But you haven't won yet."

"The kiss is to make the wager."

"But if you win you won't get a reward."

"But you said that I wouldn't."

"Stop." They were talking in circles and he was playing with her. He wasn't asking for much, just a kiss, and she was going to win. This was her chance to get out of here. This was going to be the sweetest kiss ever. This kiss would lead her home. Even in the darkness she saw the whiteness of his teeth when he smiled.

"Sure, Derek. A kiss is more than fair."

She barely finished speaking when his mouth swooped to

hers. It wasn't a cautious kiss. His lips had been there before and he knew exactly what he was doing. His kiss deepened and he moved closer to her until the length of his body pressed against hers. His tongue dipped and swirled, sending her senses into a tail-spin. All reason and logic left her. She lifted her arms around his neck; this small movement seemed to ignite him further. She was totally lost and the rest of the world disappeared, everything but the captain.

Aiyana felt his arousal pressing hard against her thigh. A shiver whipped through her and she felt an aching need growing within her.

Derek's hand slipped beneath her robe and caressed her abdomen and trailed higher. He cupped a breast and she tensed. As he gently kneaded she relaxed and yielded, wanting more. Her body was being drawn into a fire; it burned and ached with a need she had never experienced before.

His kisses trailed down her neck as he positioned himself over her and eased between her thighs. She felt pressure in her most intimate core and her eyes sprang open. Heat evaporated as she became aware this was much more than a kiss. She swam in uncharted waters and felt uncertain. Making love for the first time should be with someone she loved, not with someone who hired her, no matter how attractive he was or how good his kisses felt. As much as her body cried yes, her mind said no. Sensing her hesitation, Derek lifted his head to look at her. She realized his breathing was as erratic as hers.

"I can't," she whispered.

He moved to his side of the bed. "A kiss for a wager. Good night, Hoshikosan."

His reply had been abrupt. He probably thought she pulled away to force him to uphold the conditions of the bet. A kiss and nothing more. If only he knew why she really froze and that the wager had been the farthest thing from her mind.

This had all felt too real.

CHAPTER 10

races of the early sun shone into the room. Aiyana glanced at the captain and watched the steady rise and fall of his chest. He slept peacefully, his face looked relaxed and free of any worry. This was the first time she had ever seen him truly vulnerable. She looked at the lips that had kissed her so passionately the night before and she longed to kiss them again. But she shouldn't, no, she couldn't.

Slowly she shimmied out of bed and tiptoed to the trunks. She slipped out of her robe and put on her new shirt, pants and shoes. She took a final look back at the captain. This would be the last day she'd see him. The American ships would arrive, she'd win the bet, retrieve her comb and wake up in modern day. There was no proof this would happen but she believed it with every molecule of her being. Leaving the captain behind would be tough. She admired many qualities about him. His athleticism, his authoritative status and the way he had kissed her. An ache developed inside her chest.

She turned and burst outside into the mild dewy morning. She took deep breaths and focused on warming up with head rolls, shoulder shrugs, side bends and thigh stretches. She jogged along the same path she took yesterday that led her down to the water. The chirping birds, summer breeze and earth scents of the forest invigorated almost all her senses. When she got to the shore she dropped to her knees and splashed water on her face and neck. She scanned the bay, searching for the black ships from America, but as of yet only Derek's ship swayed in the rolling waves. She tensed with pang of doubt. What if the ships didn't arrive?

She turned and ran back up the hill and then sprinted for the final stretch to the cabin. Her muscles were warmed up and limber and she performed her kata routine of choreographed poses, punches and kicks. While taking a rest she looked out at the bay. Still no trace of black ships.

"Good morning, Hoshikosan."

Derek stood on the porch wearing only loose beige shorts. His chiseled physique disarmed her yet again. Her pulse surged and she impulsively smoothed a hand over her hair. She thought of him in bed last night and her cheeks grew hot. She had to change her train of thought.

"Did you sleep well, Captain?"

"My night was not entirely restful."

She had a feeling she knew why he didn't rest well. Not wanting Derek to see her flushed cheeks she turned away and looked out at the bay again.

"My, you're impatient for some ships to arrive," Derek said as he walked up behind her. "I can assure you that they haven't arrived yet."

He sounded annoyed. Had he thought she was so eager to get away from him?

"What are you doing out here anyway, Hoshikosan? And dressed as a boy?"

"I'm practicing martial arts. It's the reason I have to leave here." She didn't know why she added that last line of information. He squinted but said nothing.

"Captain, I've told you before, I'm preparing, training for the competition for which I came to Japan."

"The one in the future?"

"Yes, exactly. It is the reason I need my comb so I can go back and compete." Again, she felt she had to clarify she didn't want the comb returned just to get away from him, but to go to her kumite. "I was wondering, would you be interested in helping me train?" she asked hopefully.

His face lightened. "And what would that involve?"

"Come here."

She watched him step off the deck and her heart leaped at seeing his strong body's graceful strides moving toward her. He stopped close enough for her to see his warm eyes. She could stare into them forever.

"What next?"

She snapped back to the task at hand. "Well, for one, you can try blocking my punches and kicks."

"A kumite? Like before?"

"Kind of, but this time there will be no contact."

"All right." He stood solidly, fists up. "Ready."

She started maneuvering, balancing on the balls of her feet. With her usual lightning speed she threw punches and kicks in quick succession, recoiling after each combination. He did exactly as she wanted, moving and ducking away from her would-be assault.

After several rounds they paused for a break. "Where did you learn to do that? Was the Mother of the geisha house a sensei as well?"

Aiyana didn't bother to try and explain it again, it would be for nothing.

"I just have one bit of advice," he said.

What kind of advice could he mean? She was a fifth degree black belt and now felt a little indignant, no actually a lot indignant. Her technique was flawless, fast and agile. She didn't want to sound arrogant but she knew what her capabilities were. What could a sea captain from the nineteenth century have to say about modern karate?

"What's your advice, Captain? Slow down?" she asked with sarcasm.

"Yes."

She snorted. "Why? So you can hit me?"

"No. I mean for you to slow down your aggression. Truth be known, I've never seen anyone move and fight like you, not a man and especially not a woman. I dare say I am in awe of you, in more ways than one."

His voice turned sultry and a blush burned her cheeks. "Thank you."

"As I see it, you plan your attack, and because of your speed you are able to carry it out. But, you have to consider your opponent and be ready for his attack. Look at him, watch how his body moves and if you pay close attention to him you can always see an arm tense up before it is about to strike, or a body become more rigid before a kick."

"So, I just have to watch my opponent more. But, if I do that then I'll be watching him hit me."

"No, not at all. By watching or concentrating, you almost get a sense or premonition of what he will do."

"That all sounds weird."

"You just have to trust your intuition."

"I trust in my training. And how would I know if your advice really works?"

He raised a brow.

Damn. It had worked against her that night at the Temple Inn. But Aiyana wasn't about to admit it out loud. "Shall we have breakfast, Captain? I'm famished."

"Absolutely."

They went inside and sat at the table and chairs Derek had moved into the front room. "I made this furniture," he said. "My legs weren't meant to crouch and sit cross-legged on straw mats. Not all the time anyway."

Aiyana could see they weren't. "You're a carpenter as well as a sailor. I'm impressed."

He smiled and pulled out a chair for her. On the table there was a square flat dish lined with balls of rice, along with a couple of teacups and a teapot. Immediately she dove in and threw a rice ball into her mouth. She had eaten three of them before she realized Derek hadn't eaten one. "Aren't you hungry?"

"I already ate. I'll just have some tea. I have actually acquired a taste for it."

She reached over to pick up the teapot but Derek already had his hand on the handle. "I'll pour this round."

"Thank you." Her hand tingled after touching his and self-consciousness enshrouded her. Last night he had touched much more than her hand and she remembered every caress, every sensation. Something fluttered in her stomach and she looked down and focused on her food.

"Would you like a tour of my ship today?"

Aiyana chewed quickly and swallowed. "I'd love to. Old ships are really cool."

He shook his head. "It wasn't constructed very long ago so I would not classify her as old. As for being cool, it usually is on the open seas. Nonetheless, I'll get dressed and meet you out front. Today, my lovely Hoshikosan, I shall grant you a tour of the ship *Revenge*."

CHAPTER 11

*D*erek and Aiyana walked down the main road to the water front. She had a bounce in her step and couldn't wait to see Derek's ship. Until now, her life had been an unwavering routine between training and running the family business. She couldn't remember the last movie or football game she had gone to. Perhaps that was why she was so excited to do something out of the ordinary. Or, maybe it was because of who was giving the guided tour.

The sun hadn't reached its noon peak yet but it was already desert hot. They kept in stride with each other and she found herself smiling.

"You are in high spirits, Hoshikosan. Or are you withholding a grand secret?"

Aiyana kicked a stone. "I am happy but have no secrets. I've told you everything."

"Everything? I doubt that."

She wasn't sure what he meant by that so she would call him on it. "Why would you doubt it?"

"I have found that women have the ability to lock away their deepest secrets and desires and only reveal what they want you to see."

Derek's tone was light but Aiyana figured he was speaking from some sordid experience. "Well, Captain Derek, some girl has certainly played games with you. It's not right to fool around with anyone's head or heart."

"So you don't, fool around, as you just put it, Hoshikosan?"

"Nope. What you see is what you get. End of story."

He grinned. "That's good because I like what I see."

A heat wave rolled over her cheeks but it had nothing to do with the sun and everything to do with Derek. When they arrived at the water's edge they turned right and walked along the sandy shore toward a wooden rowboat tied to a short dock.

Derek hopped onto the dock then into the boat. With his feet planted wide he stood solidly in the rocking vessel and held Aiyana's hand as she climbed in after him. Once she was seated on the cross-bench Derek gave her a bright smile as he started rowing toward his ship. Now he seemed excited as a young boy showing off a new bicycle. He rowed steadily, expertly, in perfect form and without apparent effort. Water splashed off the ends of the oars each time they surfaced, only to be plunged under again and again. The refreshing breeze caressed Aiyana's damp brow and ran its invisible fingers through her hair. She stole as many glances at Derek as she could without blatantly staring.

When they neared the ship Aiyana noticed it was even larger than she had imagined. It was constructed of fine oak timber with perfect grains. Derek tied the rowboat to a ring on the ship and then they steadily climbed a rope ladder with her in the lead. Derek was at her heels, closely guarding against a possible tumble into the ocean. He helped her over the rail and onto the foredeck.

On board, two of the crewmen were mopping. They came to attention when they noticed Derek. "Ahoy, Captain!" Though they had addressed their captain their eyes were glued on Aiyana.

"Carry on, men." His order held a casual tone but the men responded immediately, putting their mops into action once again.

"Aye, aye, sir."

Aiyana inhaled the ocean breeze. She wanted to pinch herself again to ascertain she was actually on an immaculately cleaned wooden deck of a nineteenth century sailing vessel. The ship gently rocked back and forth as she looked at Tokyo harbor. Houses dotted the forested hill and much further away she saw the white cap of Mount Fuji. There were several fishing boats in the bay with the men in them busily working with their nets, either casting them or pulling in their catch.

"Come, I'll show you the ship's wheel."

They stepped up to the center of the vessel and Aiyana held the handles of the large wheel with black spokes.

"Captain, this ship is beautiful." She could tell he was beaming with pride, and so he should be.

"Thank you. It hasn't been easy to get where I am today."

She smiled and spoke wholeheartedly. "I have no doubt about that."

"Here, look through this." Derek handed her a brass telescope. "Even though we are here on a peaceful mission, someone on board is on constant watch."

Aiyana held it up her eye and focused on the glimmering deep blue waves then panned to the forest beyond the shore. "Wow, there's a great zoom on this. It looks like the shore is only ten feet away. And that tree there, I can count the leaves. Look, a fish just jumped out of the water."

"Yes, I too have watched some of the goings on along the shore and in the water."

Her mind darted back to when she had frolicked in the waves. She lowered the telescope to look at him. "Oh, really? Like what?"

"Mermaids."

He *had* seen her. She giggled and put the telescope to her eye

70

again and looked out at the horizon. As far as she could see there was only ocean. She handed the instrument back to Derek. "Captain, how did you decide to become a sailor? Was it because of all the beauty and mystery of the sea?"

"That's a good question. True, I admire everything about the ocean, its fierceness, its power, and often its tranquility. Although I love all these qualities, these are not the reasons I chose this life."

She glanced at him staring off into the distance. He seemed sad and spoke in a flat tone. "Then why?" she asked.

They heard laughter and shouts coming from the stern of the ship, then huge splashes. Aiyana looked over the railing and saw some men swimming in the ocean.

"Captain, your whole crew is jumping overboard." She laughed.

"That's not the whole lot. Only a dozen or so are staying on the ship—the ones not comfortable near samurai swords. The rest of the men are staying in Edo. Shall we go below?"

She nodded. They went below deck and continued along a narrow corridor as Derek described different areas of the ship. Next they came upon the captain's quarters. Aiyana stepped inside the masculine room with Derek behind her. The room had a wide bed with a solid wood headboard and a small round window just above it. On a long table sat a couple of candle lanterns, tankards and piles of charts, maps and nautical instruments. There was also a stack of books, on the top sat a copy of Moby Dick.

"Looks like you do a lot of studying and reading. Your table reminds me of our dining table at home. My mother uses it as an office and it's always covered with paperwork." She turned and almost planted her face into Derek's chest. "Woops, sorry, I didn't realize you were right there." But Derek didn't step back, and neither did she.

"No apology is required."

71

They stood immobile, fixed in each other's gaze. Then he moved closer, seeking her lips for a kiss, a kiss she would welcome. She felt electric excitement whenever he was near and the closer he got, the more the sparks flew. His mouth was only an inch away and her eyes fluttered shut, ready for their lips to meet. Suddenly there was a huge crash from above. Derek snapped to attention but it took her a bit longer to recompose herself.

"What the devil was that?" he said.

Derek bolted two steps at a time to the deck and she followed. At the back of the ship a couple of crewmen stood by a smashed crate and a pile of coal.

"Sorry, Captain," the stockier man said. "The crate slipped off the sling."

Derek ordered the younger sailor, who was staring at Aiyana to get another shovel. "Three of us can clean this up in no time." Derek pulled off his shirt and tossed it aside. She watched the men shovel mounds of coal onto a skid. Derek towered taller than the other two by at least half a foot. The mass of his body and broadness of his chest also greatly exceeded that of the others. His muscles tensed and flexed and his skin gleamed with perspiration. Hard work had sculpted his body to perfection.

A realization struck Aiyana. Real life and the desire to survive was the best training. This wasn't some fancy gym where guys worked out just to admire themselves in the mirror or look good on a beach. Derek probably had no idea of how incredibly attractive he was to her right now. He had a job to do and was getting it done. He had no clue that at this moment she longed for him while he was working with such determination. It felt as if her heart somehow ached for him, something she had never experienced before. Naturally she had experienced a range of emotions like extreme happiness, like on Christmas Day or when she had won her first national title, as well as sadness, when her father died. But she had never longed for anyone—not like this. Perhaps she felt such an intense feeling because this could never be. Wherever she was, she wasn't in her world. This was the first time she had feelings for a man, but this man was from the past and would never become her future.

The men finished working and Derek rested his arm on top of the shovel handle, looked at her and smiled. His eyes twinkled in the sun and areas on his tanned body were covered in soot. A black smudge ran down the side of his face and she laughed. Whether this was reality or a dream, heaven or hell, there was no question that he made her happy.

He put the shovel aside and walked over to her. "Just a minor mishap."

Aiyana smiled. "Yes, and it's all over you."

He looked down at his chest then back at her. "Then there is only one thing to do." He continued speaking as he pulled off his boots then unbuttoned his pants, slipping them off as well. "Rules of propriety state that I should be presentable in front of a lady. In my opinion that means clean." Wearing only shorts, he scooted up to the railing and hurdled over, disappearing with a splash. She peeked down and saw him treading water. He waved her in.

"Come, join me!"

The turquoise water looked inviting enough, but it was the invitation from Derek that she couldn't resist. And who never had the fantasy of jumping off a majestic ship into a clear blue ocean? She looked around at a few crewmen working. One of them smiled at her. "Go on in, miss, the captain's waiting."

She flipped off her shoes and since swimming commando was out of the question she left on her clothes. She swung her legs over the railing and paused, hanging on tight. Derek dove under out of sight for a few moments then resurfaced closer to the ship.

"Just keep your body straight when you jump."

She looked down and assessed it was at least a twelve-foot drop. Her heart beat hard. She had never even jumped off of a low diving board so this height had her concerned. She looked at Derek.

"Don't be frightened. I'm here."

Aiyana let go of the railing. She plunged deeply and it took a few seconds for her to surface. Heightened adrenaline pumped through her.

"Wow, what a rush," she said. "It's so warm and the sky is so blue. *This* is heaven."

Derek swam closer to her. "You are heaven."

She didn't want to ruin this moment by talking so she just smiled. She hoped never to forget how beautiful he was and how he made her feel happy, safe and euphoric.

"Come, I want to show you something," he said.

They swan to the rowboat. Derek hoisted himself up and in then helped lift Aiyana out of the water. Derek positioned himself on the bench and started rowing away from the ship.

"Where are we going?" Aiyana said and squeezed water out of her hair.

"Just over there, where the land jets out into the bay."

She looked over to the shore, perhaps two-hundred yards west where the water was a lighter blue. No Caribbean island could have been more beautiful or magical than this. She glanced at Derek, rowing at a strong, steady pace.

An idea popped in her head. "Can I try?"

"Try what?"

"Rowing. Can we switch seats?"

"But, why?"

"Well, for one, it's good exercise."

Derek paused and released the oars. The boat drifted and bobbed in the gentle waves. "This is hard work. But certainly you may try."

They switched spots, tilting the boat side to side as they did so. Aiyana took up the oars. It was partially a co-ordination thing to dip the oars into the water at the same time and at the same depth. The boat meandered at bit but after a few awkward tries she got the hang of it and soon she felt the burn in her biceps and lats. This workout was better than any rowing machine she had tried. Her strokes were actually moving them through the water. She looked at Derek. He put his hands behind his head and leaned back.

She laughed. "Enjoying the ride?"

"Very much so. I'd ask you to join my crew, but frankly, I don't want to share you." His face turned serious and he sat up and leaned toward her. "Not for a second, not with anyone." After a few moments he turned to fetch the anchor. "This is close enough."

Breathing heavily, Aiyana was happy for the break. They were perhaps thirty feet from shore and she looked over the boat's edge. Down below she saw the rocky ocean bottom and schools of fish. "It's lovely here, Derek. I can't believe how clean the water is."

"I like diving here. Want to see why?"

She nodded.

Suddenly the boat rocked and Derek hopped overboard. He disappeared under the water's surface and swam deeper and deeper to the bottom. He stayed below for a long time then surfaced. In his hands were what appeared to be rocks but when he swam closer she saw they were oysters. He dropped them into the boat then drove down a few more times, each time returning with handfuls of shellfish. After his last dive he climbed back into the boat.

"Now we have lunch." With a knife he pried one open. "It took me many tries before I figured out how to open these critters. Now that I have, I can never eat enough of them. Would you like this one?"

Aiyana cringed. "I have never eaten an oyster before. Don't we need lemon or hot sauce?"

He brought the half shell to his mouth, slurped and swallowed. "A taste of the ocean." He tossed the empty shell back into the water then opened another. "Here, try it."

"Okay, okay." Aiyana wasn't sure she'd be able to stomach the oyster but decided to try it, once anyway. She put the salty cup to her lips and sucked back the soft mouthful. It truly was a delicate taste of the ocean. And fresh.

"That's good," she said.

"Here, have another."

The two of them shared the rest of the oysters. When Derek opened that last one he frowned.

"What is it?" she said.

"Out of so many oysters there wasn't a single pearl."

"Well, it's no wonder, since they're not cultured."

Derek seemed confused. "What do you mean?"

"Oh, I guess you wouldn't know. You can culture pearls by embedding a speck of sand into the mollusk. To protect itself from the so-called intruder, the oyster builds layers of nacre around the foreign body thereby creating an iridescent gem."

Derek laughed. "If that were true then that wouldn't make a pearl very rare, would it?"

"I guess not." The afternoon sun was unbearably hot and Aiyana impulsively jumped into the water. She swam on her back and looked up. There were sparse clouds in the blue sky and the occasional bird flew by. She closed her eyes to totally feel the sun's rays and the ocean's caress. This was pure bliss. She heard a splash. While still floating on her back she felt arms cradling her. She opened her eyes and saw Derek's handsome face, glistening with wetness. His mouth found hers in a light salty kiss. She moved to tread water and his hands circled her waist. He pulled her closer for another kiss, one she willingly gave, one she was robbed of on the ship. She playfully pushed away from him.

"Race you to shore."

She had a head start and didn't look back. With all the racing speed she had she swam forward. When she reached the shore she looked back. She had beaten him by half a body length. She sat on the sandy shore with her feet still dipped in the water. "I beat you."

Derek positioned himself beside her and shook his head before looking at her. "Yes you did, my competitive geisha."

Her heart thumped strongly from the swim and kept up the pace from having Derek so close. He was genetically perfect. And more importantly, they connected. She inched closer to him and wiped some water off his cheek. He put his arm around her and she shivered.

He rubbed her upper arm. "Cold?" He said with concern lacing his voice.

"No," she said. It was he who was making her shiver. She lifted her chin and moved her face closer to his. She wanted more of the kiss he had given her in the ocean—much more. When their lips connected she immediately felt passion's heat. First on her lips then throughout her body. Slowly they lay back on the sand and Derek moved her to be on top of him.

With her legs on either side of him, Aiyana leaned over and boldly kissed his lips, face and neck and moved a trail to his chest. She felt his sudden intake of air. His hands caressed her back and waist then moved to her belly and up along her abdomen and breasts. Through the thin wet fabric she felt his fingers against her nipples. The pleasure from his fondling only made her yearn for more. She dropped forward to press her body against the length of his.

She didn't care where she was, brazenly kissing a sailor on a beach. Right now all she wanted to do was satisfy a raging fire burning deep within her. These feelings were foreign and strong and she didn't know how to deal with them. Did she feel this way because of the oysters? She certainly didn't need aphrodisiacs with a man like Derek. She started unbuttoning her shirt .She undid two buttons then stopped.

Aiyana looked at Derek's passion-laden face and into his

smoky green eyes. She wanted to remember him and this moment forever. Suddenly there was a loud rumbling bang in the distance. Derek sat up while holding her close. They looked out in the direction from where the noise came.

Out in the ocean, sailing in from the horizon were ships. Black ships, belching black smoke. One, two, three, four.

Commodore Matthew Perry's fleet from America had arrived.

CHAPTER 12

With the arrival of the American fleet, Derek and Aiyana's attention was pulled out to sea, halting their romantic interlude. Aiyana slid off Derek's lap and sat next to him and while the rhythmic whooshing sound of the ocean filled her ears they focused on the horizon. This event had occurred over 150 years ago yet here she was, on the beach with waves lapping her feet, watching historical scenes more real than an *Imax* movie. The ships moved closer and the black clouds of smoke grew larger. Aiyana shivered with excitement and anticipation.

"Aren't they magnificent? They arrived, just like I said they would." She turned to look at Derek. His expression was dark. Was he angry? "Derek, what's wrong?"

"Are wagers and winning all that matter to you?"

Aiyana froze. Only a few short minutes ago he was kissing her with that perfect mouth but now he was using it to sting her with words.

"What do you mean?"

"I suppose you are happy because you will be getting your comb back?"

While being enthralled at the arrival of Commodore Perry's ships Aiyana hadn't thought of that, until now. "Well, yes. That was the deal."

"A deal I didn't make." His voice was clipped with iciness. He stepped out into the water and when it was too deep to wade any further he dove under and swam toward the small boat.

Aiyana stood in shock. This might have been the most amazing day of her life—she was about to make love to the man of her dreams, only to be interrupted by a monumental moment in history. Now she was trying to unravel what had gone wrong. Derek was angry and she was going to find out why.

She splashed into the water after him but he beat her by far. This made her realize he had let her win the race before. By the time she swam to the boat her lungs burned and she clung onto the side of the craft to catch her breath. Derek just sat there and held the oars. He ignored her and didn't even attempt to help her out of the water, not that she would have accepted. It took her a couple of tries to lift her leg and hook it over the side of the boat, then with great effort she pulled her concrete weight over and in. She thumped like a heavy fish. Immediately he started rowing toward his ship like a maniac, his tempo double-time.

She clenched her hands on either side of the boat and at the moment the warm sun and ocean breeze gave her no comfort. "What the hell is wrong with you? Derek, look at me." But he didn't, he just kept rowing. Ideas flashed through her mind. There could be two possible reasons. First, perhaps he was annoyed because she was right about the arrival of the ships and had proven him wrong. But, she didn't think his ego was that fragile or that he would be so childish and insecure.

Second, and more likely, he was mad that she wanted her comb back so she could leave here, and leave him. Whether he truly believed about the 'power of the comb' or not was another story. But he was aware that the hair ornament was sentimental to her and she would not leave it behind. That was probably it.

He had paid for a geisha and expected her to uphold her part of the bargain. She would try to explain.

"Derek, would you at least look at me?" All at once he stopped laboring and finally acknowledged her. His brows were low over his brilliant greenish eyes and his expression appeared pained, tormented. She felt heaviness in her chest. "Please, Derek, understand that I am not a geisha and I need to get home." She looked at the turquoise waves that gently rocked their boat and then scanned the lush green shore. "But, it's so beautiful here. I'm realizing that the more time I spend with you, the less I want to leave." Her voice had become a whisper.

Derek's expression softened. "And the more I am with you the more I realize that you belong with me. Hoshikosan, sail home with me."

Her emotions felt like turbulent clouds whirling within her. "I can't." She realized that her focus had shifted away from the competition and that was unacceptable to her. It would be easy to abandon her goals to a man like Derek. Also, even more importantly, if she decided to stay with the captain her mother would have lost a daughter as well as a husband. This would be too much agony for her mother to bear, especially since they had parted after an argument without any resolution.

Derek resumed rowing, this time at a normal pace. Without any other exchange of words they travelled back to the ship and climbed the unsteady rope ladder up to the deck. Derek went over to where he had left his clothes and pulled on his shirt. A few sailors rushed over to eagerly talk to their captain about what was happening not a mile away. Aiyana strolled over to the railing and put on her shoes. Although she and the captain were apart, they connected by catching glimpses of one another, each acutely aware of the other's movements.

"They're something else, aren't they?"

Aiyana turned to the crewman beside her who had just

spoken. He had a head of tight black curls and a pleasant smile framed by a thick beard.

"My name is Sean Bradford, first mate."

"Hello. My name is Aiyana, though people here call me Hoshikosan." She held out her hand. When he looked at her outstretched hand he glanced around before he proceeded to shake it. Aiyana gave him a firm hand shake and he raised his brows and smiled.

"Your slender hand has the grip of a vice, Miss Aiyana."

"Thank you." She appreciated the compliment but even more so, she liked being called by her real name. "You don't sound like you have a Dutch accent, Sean. Are you American as well?"

"Aye. There are a handful of us on the *Revenge*. Truth be told, we'd sail for the captain under any flag."

Derek came up behind them and dropped an appreciative hand on Sean's shoulder.

Their attention was drawn to the land, where alarms sounded. Visibly, more and more people gathered along the shore. Aiyana noticed the nearby fisherman had pulled in their nets and rowed frantically to land, away from the approaching fleet.

"Look at that," Sean said while looking at the beach. "They're panicked, racing every which way."

"What do we do now, Captain?" Sean asked.

"It is obvious all hell has broken loose on shore."

"Even without cell phones, by now half of the city probably knows of Captain Perry's arrival."

Sean narrowed his eyes. "Cell phones?"

"Yes, they're a means of communication in the fut—" She stopped herself from finishing. Derek glared at her and Sean still looked confused. "Um, I'll tell you later."

The four black ships steamed closer and moved alongside them. Derek and his crew saluted the Americans on deck as they moved past. Aiyana's mouth slackened in awe and then she grabbed the railing as the ship rocked in their wake. The Americans moved closer shore and dropped anchor. All the ships pointed a multitude of cannons toward the coast.

"Sean, Hoshikosan and I must return to shore. We can't risk not being allowed back into the country. Stay on high alert as to the turn of events."

"Understood, Captain."

"Good-bye, Sean. It was nice meeting you."

"And you, my lady." Sean bowed before the couple walked away.

Aiyana and Derek climbed back down into the small boat and rowed to shore. On the beach they walked passed people who seemed to be both scared and excited at the same time. Aiyana heard a man yell. "Look at the giant dragons puffing smoke." Beside her a young woman pulled her hat lower with trembling hands crying. "They're alien ships of fire."

Aiyana stopped and put her hand on the woman's shoulder. "No, they're not alien. They're just men who have sailed from another land but mean no harm."

The teary eyed woman looked up at Aiyana. "They have come to destroy our sacred land." She turned and weaved back into the crowd.

"Derek, this is the first time these people have seen steamships. No wonder they're alarmed."

"Yes, that's true. Come, let's get away from here. I don't like those guns pointing at us." The captain took her hand and she followed him as they weaved their way off the shore and up the steep grassy hill. On a plateau that offered a clear view of the bay and coast they sat down.

Aiyana leaned toward Derek. "Isn't all this exciting?"

"You call mass chaos and impending murder, exciting?" His jaw clenched.

"It's the history in the making I find exciting. There is the father of the Steam Navy. And Derek, as far as I remember, no one is murdering anyone."

"And you know all this from the future?"

"Yes."

His eyes met hers. He looked like he wanted to believe her, and then she noticed slight movements of his head from side to side. "Impossible."

Temple bells echoed in the distance. It appeared that she and Derek were at an impasse yet again. He'd never believe where, but more importantly, when she was from.

He wore a stony expression.

"What's wrong?" she asked.

He looked at her with sad eyes and her heart hurt. "I don't take failure well, Hoshikosan?"

"Failure? What do you mean?"

He ran a hand through his hair. "By now all of Edo must know the Americans are here. No doubt the Commodore will meet with the shogun soon and all I can do is sit and watch."

"Yes they will meet, but what does that have to do with you?"

"My dear woman, I have been here for almost a month and still have not been able to meet with the shogun. Soon I will be forced to leave and not have done what I had set out to accomplish." He slammed a fist into the ground.

CHAPTER 13

*A*iyana slapped a mosquito on her arm as she looked at the Japanese military's torches on the beach. A hundred men, maybe two or three hundred, had congregated. It was hard to see through the darkness but it seemed it had become quiet and uneventful down below.

"It's doubtful anything more will happen until tomorrow," Derek said. He reached out his hand to help her up and she welcomed it. Her body felt heavy as lead. The day's strenuous events had caught up with her. With the lack of light, their trek back to the cabin through thick brush and woods was challenging. The sound of chirping crickets filled the quiet night and the distinctive sound took her back to her childhood. On balmy evenings such as these she used to sit on the porch with her father. She loved hearing the sound of his voice as he told her stories. Those times were worry free and filled with hope.

She took a deep breath in and out and then focused on the final steep rocky climb. Derek cupped her elbow and guided her upward. It was a caring gesture and helped ease the heaviness of her heart, more than he'd ever know. She bet if he lived in modern days he would insist on opening and closing the car door for her. Maybe he'd even carry her gym bag.

Derek still wasn't himself; he hadn't said two words since they started walking back. It seemed he was taking his monumental quest too personally. He should deduce that Commodore Perry's arrival proved it would only be a matter of time before the borders opened. What Derek wanted would happen, eventually. It just needed time. He should be encouraged negotiations would eventually get underway.

Their pace slowed as they approached the house. Boldly, Aiyana took one of Derek's hands into hers. "Come, let's sit and you can tell me what's been rattling around in your brain."

Derek turned up a corner of his mouth. "Rattling in my brain? Trust me, Hoshikosan, you do not want to know."

She pulled him toward the front stairs. "Oh, but I do. Right down to the last nut and bolt."

"Unfortunately I cannot stay here right now."

"Why? Where do you have to go?"

He moved closer and his cheek brushed hers. Her heart leaped. She felt his warm breath in her hair then a silent kiss. His hand slipped out of hers.

"I do not know how long I will be gone. But stay close to the house." Derek backed away then disappeared into the night.

She looked after him into blackness.

What are you up to, Derek?

Aiyana went inside and took off her shoes. Mariko was drawing by lantern light and when she noticed Aiyana she dropped her pencil and stood.

"No, Mariko, don't get up. Keep doing what you're doing. I'm just going to bed. Goodnight."

"Goodnight, Hoshikosan."

Aiyana went straight to her room and thought she had been somewhat rude to Mariko. She could have at least asked the girl how her day was or what she thought about the American ships.

She would apologize to Mariko tomorrow. After peeling off her clothes and slipping on a silk robe Aiyana crawled into bed. She pulled up the covers only to kick them off seconds later. She flipped and turned. On her back she stared straight up into the darkness. For how long she didn't know. Thoughts circled in her head.

Kumite, mom, home, Derek, comb.

She didn't know when she fell asleep but it was still dark when she awoke. Not wanting to stare into idle darkness again, she got up and padded barefoot outside. A warm wind made her robe dance and flap like a merry flag. She sat on the top step and looked up. The sky was black, dotted with countless stars. She guessed it was somewhere around four in the morning.

Where was Derek? What was he doing at this hour? Surely it had something to do with the arrival of the American ships. Aiyana didn't like being in any form of darkness. Suddenly, out of nowhere, a blue meteor with a red tail flew across the sky, leaving a trail of exploding sparks. She blinked only when it was gone and then stood with renewed determination.

"Tonight's the first and last night you leave me in the dark, Captain Blackburn, because tomorrow I'm going to find out what you're up to."

CHAPTER 14

*D*uring the remaining hours of the night Aiyana often checked beside her but found she was still alone in bed. Derek had been gone the entire night. Where was he? Had he gone to the beach?

With the first rays of the sun Aiyana sprang up to get the day started. She pulled on a pair of Capri pants and a short-collard white shirt and peeked inside Mariko's room. Once again Aiyana requested Mariko's assistance. The girl agreed to help with Aiyana's plan and quickly left the cabin to get the deed done. Aiyana went outside and glanced around. The fresh morning air invigorated her like a cool shower as did the view overlooking the beach. Hundreds of Japanese guard boats dotted the bay and surrounded Commodore Perry's fleet. The shoreline was crowded with Japanese military and hordes of curious watchers.

She paced. Mariko's help was vital for Aiyana's plan. More than anything she wanted to go down to the shore and get a better view of the ships and people on the beach. But she couldn't, not yet. Meanwhile she started her exercise regime. She stretched and performed a kata of choreographed patterns containing combat techniques, kicks and punches. She made her movements strong and precise and breathed deeply from the diaphragm. She exhaled in a finishing bent-knee pose and noticed Mariko standing a few feet from her. The girl's mouth was open.

"Mariko, you're back," Aiyana said and straightened up. "Is everything set to go?"

"Yes, my brother is around here somewhere."

Aiyana clasped her hands together. "Great."

Mariko tilted her head to the side. "Hoshikosan, what were you just doing?"

"That was called kata."

"For what purpose is kata?"

"Well." Aiyana wiped her brow with the bottom of her shirt. "Self-defense for one thing."

"You have a danna. He will defend you."

"True, but who will defend me from my danna?" Aiyana didn't know if Mariko understood her sense of humor. The girl always said so little and remained formal. Though she was extremely polite she acted too serious for her age and needed to lighten up.

"Mariko, do you want to learn some moves?" Mariko didn't answer. Just when Aiyana thought this idea was a lost cause the girl smiled and nodded.

"Great. Put down that huge basket and come here." Mariko did as she was told. "Okay, now think, was there any time when someone attacked you or did something to you and you couldn't fight back?"

Mariko thought for a moment. "Yes, last year."

"What happened?"

"I was walking home through the field after being at the market. My basket was very heavy, filled with fruit, eggs and rice. Then suddenly someone seized me from behind. Arms squeezed around my body and when I dropped my basket the thief stole it."

"That's terrible. Now, re-enact it and I'll show you what you could have done."

From behind, Mariko wrapped her arms around Aiyana. Aiyana then lightly stomped on Mariko's foot, bent forward to bump into Mariko to knock her off balance and then reached down to pulled one of Mariko's legs forward between her own. Mariko fell backwards onto her rear. "I see," was all she said.

Aiyana helped her up. "Now you try." She stood behind Mariko and wrapped her arms around the girl. Without warning, Mariko firmly stomped on her foot, bumped back into Aiyana and grabbed her ankle, flipping her back. From the ground Aiyana looked up and despite her smarting foot she started laughing. The girl was a natural. Mariko began giggling as well, covering her mouth with her hand.

"See, Mariko, next time no one will touch your basket. And don't cover your smile." She pulled Mariko's hand down. "You have a beautiful smile."

"Thank you, Hoshikosan. I must do my work now." She went over to the basket she had put down.

"What do you have to do?"

"Ikebona."

The art of flower arranging. "Mind if I watch?"

Mariko smiled and eagerly nodded. They sat at a table beneath the scanty shade of a locus tree, Mariko carefully laid out wood chips, rocks, tree branches and summer flowers. She placed a square pottery dish in front of her and a round one in front of Aiyana.

Aiyana glanced around for Derek but saw no sign of him. She looked at the dish in front of her. "Wait, you want me to make an arrangement?"

Mariko nodded.

"No, Mariko, I'm not creative."

"Yes you are, Hoshikosan. I saw you dancing your kata."

Aiyana smiled. "All right, I'll try."

"First we layer rocks and wood chips. They represent the earth and must ground everything else."

Aiyana arranged pebbles and wood fragments in the dish and tried to make them look as symmetrical as Mariko's.

"Next we stand up the wood branches in the earth to reach heaven. Then we add flowers to symbolize people and the harmony between heaven and earth."

Harmony. Aiyana couldn't remember the last time anything in her life was harmonious, yet it was what she wanted. The last encounter with her mother was anti-harmonious. She wouldn't support Aiyana's decision to compete and for the first time since her father died, Aiyana walked out on her mom without a hug or a good-bye.

Aiyana inserted several branches into her arrangement and randomly added purple and white flowerets.

Mariko nodded happily. "That is lovely, Hoshikosan."

Aiyana laughed. Her arrangement looked like an overgrown jungle compared to Mariko's fine masterpiece. "I think I used too much wood."

"A lot of wood is good. It smells nice and shows warmth," Mariko said encouragingly. "You know, a tree has two lives. The first when it is alive, the second after if falls."

Two lives... Aiyana pondered the thought.

Movement drew her attention to the left. Derek took long strides toward them. He had dark lines on his face and wore a serious expression.

"Hoshikosan, Mariko, get back!"

Automatically Aiyana looked toward the bay. While working with Mariko she hadn't noticed the flurry of activity on the decks of the American ships. Suddenly, there were deep rumbling explosions from the ship cannons. Derek jumped in front of Aiyana and Mariko then pushed them to the dirt. For several minutes the earth shook as cannon balls shelled land and destroyed buildings. Mariko squealed and covered her ears. On the ground Aiyana looked at Derek with wide eyes. When the bombing stopped they got up and Mariko scrambled into the house. In the harbor smoke hovered over the water like an eerie fog and traces of burnt gunpowder laced the air. The Japanese boats surrounding the American squadron began dispersing.

"That was crazy," Aiyana said, her heart still beat fiercely.

"The Americans are refusing to be intimidated," Derek said with a far-away look.

She turned to him. "You showed up here like a raging bull. You knew what was going to happen, didn't you?"

He rubbed his neck. "I knew it might happen. Last night we rowed to the Saratoga—the American ship closest to mine. We found out Commodore Perry is demanding permission to deliver a letter from President Millard Fillmore."

"And he will," Aiyana said.

"How are you so certain?" With vibrant green eyes Derek looked at her. "How did you know exactly when the Americans would arrive? And more importantly, how are you predicting the outcome? Are you some sort of witch?"

"Witch? I don't think so."

He looked more intently at her. "You must be because you've bewitched me. By your beauty, your words, your kisses. You are unlike anyone I've known."

Aiyana wanted to tell him how she felt but something held her back. She tore her gaze from his and looked down. "Oh, I'm not so different." I'm just from a different time she wanted to say. It was futile to try and explain again.

He reached out and traced his fingertips along her cheek. "But you are different." He moved closer, his lips only inches from hers. "You are rarer and more elusive than a single pearl in the vast ocean." His lips touched hers in a tender kiss. He pulled away and paused before he spoke, as if trying to recompose himself. "I won't be back again tonight. My men and I have more business to tend to."

"Business? At night?" Derek didn't explain so she probed further. "What are you doing? Why are you really here in Japan?"

Derek's attention was led somewhere behind her. She turned and saw a middle-aged man with straight posture in an imperial uniform. He had a rolled up scroll in his hand.

"Are you, Hoshikosan, from the house of Nakahara?"

Aiyana nodded. "Yes."

He handed her the scroll. "From Shogun Ieyoshi." Then he bowed and backed away.

Derek's eyes widened. "Open it," he said in a tight voice.

Slowly she unrolled the thick textured paper. Written in black calligraphy was an invitation requesting her presence to perform a tea ceremony for the shogun.

"What does it say?"

"It's an invitation to the shogun's castle tomorrow. Do you know what this means, Derek? I can try to set up a meeting between the two of you. This is our chance."

"Our?" he said in a softer voice.

"I mean, your chance. Or, I could try to convince him of the benefits of opening Japan to the rest of the world, especially America."

"No. I have to see him myself."

Aiyana backed up. He was incensed. Did he not trust a woman to do a man's job? She scoffed. Things weren't so different in the future. "Okay, Derek, whatever you say. I'll do my best to get you in."

"In exchange for what?" He narrowed his eyes.

What he said just sank in and she couldn't refuse this opportunity.

"The same wager as before, Derek. A meeting with the shogun for my comb."

He clenched his jaw and nodded. "At any cost or any wager. Get me into Edo Palace and the comb is yours."

CHAPTER 15

*A*iyana crept backward across the porch and when Derek's silhouette disappeared into the woods she ran inside the house.

"Mariko, he's gone. Are you sure your brother is going to follow him?"

In the kitchen Mariko chopped veggies. "Yes, Hoshikosan, I am sure."

"Okay, perfect. Here, let me assist you, Mariko. It will help pass the time."

Together they finished cooking a meal, tidied the house and swept the floor. They went outside to shake out mats and saw a thin young man running towards them.

"Katsumi!" Mariko said and rushed down the porch to hug her brother. He breathed heavily from running and his short hair glistened with perspiration. "Are you all right. You've been gone for hours. Hoshikosan, this is my brother, Katsumi."

"Nice to meet you," Aiyana said and the teenager bowed. He had an oval face, smooth skin and dark chocolate eyes. "Do you know where the captain went?" Aiyana asked, cutting the formalities short.

"Yes," he said. "I lost him because he had a horse and carriage, but later I discovered he was at the Shirabyoshi Teahouse with several of his crew men."

Aiyana wrinkled her brow. "They went for tea?"

"Yes," Katsumi said, finally breathing more normally. "And there are maiko dancers there as well."

Aiyana's body tensed. "The city is frantic and he goes for tea and a lap dance?"

"Hoshikosan," Mariko said. "You should know the shogun's councilors, the bakufu, often go to that tea house."

"Now *that* makes sense." Aiyana turned to Katsumi and hugged him. "Thank you for finding this out for me."

He looked down shyly and nodded.

"Come, Hoshikosan, let's get you ready. And Katsumi, get a drink of water before you collapse."

In her bedroom, Aiyana sat on a chair and tried not to fidget while Mariko combed her hair.

"Let's leave it down tonight," Aiyana said.

"As you wish. It will flow free like shimmering silk." Mariko applied the translucent white foundation, dramatic black eyeliner and sensual red lip color. The final step was the gown. Aiyana chose a crimson kimono, dark to blend in with the darkness of the night. Mariko handed her a fan and Aiyana opened and waved it.

Mariko shook her head. "Hoshikosan, you are too beautiful not to be noticed with or without the fan."

Aiyana slipped her feet into the geta. "I'll stay in the shadows as much as I can. Now, wish me luck."

A rickshaw took her into the lantern-lit town. They drove down a narrow alleyway before arriving at a simple, rectangular wooden building. She stepped off the vehicle and clutched the fan tightly. The aroma of food mixed with the heavy humid air. She decided to peek inside the front window before entering. At the very back an empty stage was lit up and the other three walls were lined with low tables and patrons sitting on cushions. Some men were deep in conversation while others gazed at geisha fluttering about them.

She couldn't see Derek until she looked down and saw him sitting right under her. She jumped back and slammed into a man walking by.

"Oh, pardon me," she said. The man bowed and apologized as well. She shimmied to the window again and put her ear to where it was opened a crack. All she heard were muffled noises from the crowd. She had to get closer but couldn't from out here. She'd go inside, hold the fan over her face and sit at the table next to Derek with her back to him. This way she'd hear his conversation. Maybe by some small miracle she could pull this off without being noticed.

Aiyana went to the back of the building to search for a discreet entrance. She found a doorway and stepped inside. A short corridor led her to what seemed to be back stage. A few ladies scurried about and someone grabbed her arm and pulled her forward.

"There you are," the older woman said. "The music has started, now go."

The woman had mistaken her for a maiko dancer. In an instant Aiyana was pushed through a curtain onto the stage and her plan to enter the teahouse unnoticed was a bust. Lights brightened and she snapped the fan in front of her face and peeked out over it at the audience. Someone started plucking the three-stringed shamisen and the attentive audience was waiting for her to dance. Her heart beat wildly as the instrument's sound vibrated in her ears. She turned to run off the stage and then heard applause—there was going to be a lot of disappointed people. But, as much as she wanted to vacate the stage she didn't. The music now sliced the silence of the air and she felt the tunes deep inside of her.

Instead of taking two steps off the stage she took two steps to center stage. She looked at Derek. He was no longer immersed in conversation, his attention was on her. She was used to performing in front of people, but in a ring, and not in front of Derek. Tonight was totally different. In a snap decision she decided to perform her kata on stage, to music.

Aiyana bowed to the crowd. She moved the fan from her face and swept it outward as she raised her arms in a high-karate pose. Gracefully she stepped through a kata routine, flipping her arms and fan in full movements, keeping with the tempo of the music. Slow when the music slowed, crisp when the music picked up. Before she knew it her movements interpreted the music and she became an artistic embodiment of the instrument's sounds. She reached, pulled, stretched and pivoted. When the strings slowed so did she. With the final plucks she softly dropped to her knees, closed her eyes and butterflied the fan in front of her.

It took a few moments for the crowd's resonating applause to pull Aiyana out of her trance. She stood and bowed, and then saw Derek across the room. He wasn't smiling. She bowed a final time and backed off the stage. Once behind the curtain the realization of her actions sunk in. She trembled and wiped away a few tears. And then she giggled. For the first time in her life she felt deeply connected to her Japanese heritage. She wiped away another tear and thought of her father. He was here in the deepest part of her soul and she felt him through music and dance.

"That was magic, Hoshikosan," said the woman who had pushed her on stage. "Now, your company has been requested by the shogun's councilor and his men. Please join them as soon as possible."

Aiyana bowed and her thoughts raced as the woman walked away from her. This evening was turning out better than she had anticipated. First she'd go to Derek's table and tell him who had requested her presence. That would give him an opportunity to tell her what he was planning.

She entered the restaurant and heads snapped in her direction and people applauded. She bowed and then with dainty steps glided across the room to where the captain sat. She lowered her eyes as she kneeled beside him and then glanced over. He still wore an unsmiling, unreadable expression. Perhaps the slight crease on his brow displayed concern.

"Your dance was enchanting, Hoshikosan."

"Thank you, Captain."

"But I must say, I didn't expect to see you here."

She shrugged. "Surprise."

"Yes, it is," Derek said. "Here are a few members of my crew—Nate, Sal and you remember Sean?"

She smiled. "Yes, of course. Good evening, gentlemen."

"Miss Hoshikosan," Sean said. "When you moved that fan to the fine plucking of that instrument I got gooseflesh like a fat, bald turkey."

She laughed. "You're too kind." Before she could say another word another geisha wearing a cobalt blue kimono kneeled beside her.

"The councilor has requested you join him immediately," she said in a hushed tone.

The captain leaned forward. "The councilor will be disappointed because Hoshikosan is leaving." He stood, stepped over the low table and like a whirlwind, escorted Aiyana outside. In front of the teahouse he released her arm.

She adjusted her sleeve. "What's your hurry?"

"What are you doing here?" he said.

Aiyana twitched and felt like she was getting in trouble for being out after the street lights went on. "I'm not a child."

The captain scrunched puzzled eyebrows. "Who said you were?"

"Well you're treating me like one."

"If that is the case, madame, it's because I didn't want that letch, or any other letch, ogling you. As far as I'm concerned you are off the market."

Aiyana snorted. "Captain, I was never on the market."

He moved forward and pulled her into his arms. His lips met hers in fierce urgency. His lips were warm and lush like velvet of the meadows yet he came upon her with the suddenness of a storm. She hadn't expected this passionate attack and instinctively recoiled and stepped back. Her heart beat wildly and although she enjoyed his warm mouth on hers all this high emotional intensity frightened her. It was so new, and so strong.

In the shadows of flickering light, Derek stared at her. Hurt or angry, she couldn't tell. How could she? When she was around him she herself didn't know what to feel. He could make her angry, yet she had respect for him. And when he was close to her he sent her senses racing and caused all logic to become obscured in her brain.

The sound of scuffling feet caught their attention. The captain's men came out of the teahouse.

"Captain, they're leaving."

Without hesitation, Derek took Aiyana's hand and led her to the rickshaw. "You must go."

She stepped up and sat in. "Where are you going? Please, I must know."

He looked intently at her. "All will be revealed in due time." Derek spoke to the rickshaw runner, handed him some yen and Aiyana was off. She looked back to only to see Derek disappear into the night. Again.

CHAPTER 16

The formerly peaceful beachfront was now transformed into a nineteenth century Japanese military base. She stood on the hilltop and watched the activities below. The sandy shoreline was filled with hundreds of soldiers, maybe thousands, and the soothing sound of the surf was drowned out by the shouts of commanding officers.

Aiyana sat on a patch of grass and wrapped her arms around her bent knees. She was no expert on weaponry but she knew that the natives below carrying spears, bows and arrows didn't stand a chance against the American guns and cannons. She looked into the harbor at the four American ships and further back to the right at Derek's.

She had no clue as to what hour he had gotten in last night because for the first time since she arrived in this place she had a solid slumber. Perhaps she was exhausted from sensory overload —her debut dance at the teahouse, the pending meeting with the shogun and Derek's fervent kiss.

She couldn't watch from afar any more. She stood and weaved her way down the hill to the shore. There was still time before she had to meet with the shogun and her curiosity wouldn't let her stay away any longer.

Aiyana walked along the periphery. At this closer view she saw archers and samurai warriors in ferocious looking masks. The masks, feathered bows and rusty spears weren't nearly as scary as the artillery in the bay pointed in their direction.

Many people around her weren't military, just curious watchers. Several artists were busy drawing on rolls of rice paper with fine brushes and ink stones. Aiyana stopped to watch a slim, elderly man sketching in quick strokes. She cast a shadow across his drawing and he turned to look at her.

"That's a beautiful sketch of the ships—very representative."

He bowed his head.

"Do you have any more?"

He smiled and revealed a dark gap where a front tooth was missing. "Yes, many." He proudly flipped through several sketches of the American ships at different angles and of people on shore. Then he showed her a drawing of an American sailor. "Look at this hairy barbarian. His face is covered in fur."

Aiyana laughed and put herself in the man's point of view. Aside from having scalp hair, the Japanese were relatively hairless. Seeing men with mounds of facial and body hair was probably quite shocking to them.

"Have you been on the beach long?" she said.

"Since they arrived."

She looked out to sea and noticed no interaction with the Americans and Japanese. "Have any Americans come to shore?"

"Not a one. I've heard they won't talk to anyone but the shogun."

She slapped a palm to her forehead. "Shogun. Thanks for showing me those but I've got to run." She sprinted along the beach, no easy task when her feet sank with every step while trying to dodge around people. Trekking up the hill she pushed through fatigue and only stopped when she got to the cabin. She pulled air deeply into her lungs and tried to slow her respiration.

Mariko paced when Aiyana entered the house.

"Hoshikosan, we must work quickly."

Aiyana sat on a chair while Mariko applied make-up. "Is the captain still sleeping?"

"Yes," Mariko said. "He was out most of the night."

Zoning out, Aiyana thought about what Edo Palace would look like inside and how her meeting would transpire with the shogun. And, if everything went according to plan, she'd be going home.

Mariko twisted Aiyana's hair and fastened it up with two red lacquered sticks. As a final touch Mariko pinned a bloom of a rare white dahlia behind her ear. Mariko held a mirror in front of Aiyana. The reflection was startling and Aiyana would never get used to seeing herself like this. Powdered white skin, coal lash line and cherry lips. She looked like a genuine geisha, that is, except for her eyes. Mariko helped Aiyana into a passion red kimono and a pure yellow obi symbolizing sacredness. Aiyana looked up and saw Derek frozen in the doorway. His tunic hung loosely over his pants and gaped open revealing his pec muscles. Her heart leaped. He was handsome to be sure, but his absolute maleness and confidence in everything he said and did captivated her.

"You are a vision for the gods, Hoshikosan," he said.

His complement knocked air out of her. "Thank you, Captain. I want you to know I will do all I can to set up a meeting with you and the shogun. Hopefully all Mariko's preparatory work has not been for nothing."

"Oh, trust me, Hoshikosan, already it has served a purpose."

She hoped her blush didn't match the shade of her kimono though it felt like it did. What happened next was up to her. She would have to be persuasive and act appropriately. Her future depended on it.

The captain walked her to the imperial carriage waiting on the road. The driver stood beside the horse and held it by the bit. Derek took one of Aiyana's hands and enfolded it in his.

"For many reasons I shall be waiting most impatiently for your return."

She looked into his turbulent hazel eyes. "Wish me luck."

"Nay, you will make your luck. And don't hesitate to defend yourself if need be." He winked.

She laughed. "I hope it doesn't come to that."

He helped her into the carriage and the driver jumped up onto the front bench and flicked the reins. She waved as they drove away. She was bounced and jarred as they rolled along the country road then onto the stone road to Edo. After what felt like an hour on a paint shaker, in the clearing she saw the Tokugawa Shogun's Palace—a modest building in quiet woods surrounded by watch towers. The horse clip-clopped on the wooden bridge over a moat. When she had been here last with Derek it had been at night. There was definitely more to see in day light. They entered the grounds through the heavy door of the Ottoman Gate into an immaculately manicured garden. To the right was a large kidney shaped pond with lily pads and golden carp. Bushes of pink and white flowers and evergreen shrubs guided their path to the palace.

The wagon gave a final lurch and the driver helped Aiyana down. She walked up to the giant dark oak door. A male servant let her in through the wide doorway into a foyer with parquet flooring. Overhead loomed a tall ceiling of gold patterned tiles and a large chandelier. To the left he led her to a room and told her to wait. While waiting she looked around. The whole wall on her right consisted of a beautiful color drawing of a garden with rocks, bushes and cherry trees with full pink blossoms. On another wall was a mural of the city of Edo outlined in gold. In the center of the room a lantern sat on a low square oak table surrounded by pink, gold and orange cushions. She paced the room and stopped at one end and examined a stone, two-foot Amida Buddha.

After about ten minutes of pacing, a short man finally entered. He wore a copious black robe and had shiny slick hair to match. This was a bakufu, a councilor to the shogun. After seeing his high forehead Aiyana recognized him from the Tanabata Festival and from the tea house last night. *This was an odd coincidence.* The bakufu held a lot of power and helped rule the country. Perhaps he would interview her before taking her to the shogun.

Aiyana bowed slowly and kept her eyes on his. He also bowed.

"I am Hoshikosan, here at the shogun's request."

"We shall sit."

He went over to the cushions on the floor and sat down. Obediently Aiyana followed and only knelt when he motioned her to do so. She felt unsettled by him. He didn't smile or frown and just turned up his flaring nostrils and wore a snobbish expression. She thought he'd never speak until he finally opened his mouth.

"You knew about the black ships. How?"

This was a loaded question. She couldn't tell him the truth. He'd lock her away for being insane. She'd try to provide the most plausible explanation.

"I heard a rumor that the Americans were coming."

He pressed his lips together before speaking. "From who? The Dutch captain?"

"Ah—yes. His crew heard word from ships farther west." She just made this up.

"Spies?"

Aiyana wasn't sure how to answer. "I don't think so."

"Are you a spy?"

"No."

"Then why do you not lower your eyes when you speak?" He reached to stroke a bony finger down her cheek. Her body stiffened and it took great effort not to recoil from his icy touch. "You look like a geisha, the most beautiful that I have seen, but you act differently."

She lowered her eyes.

"Are you learning foreign ways from the Dutchman?"

She shot him a look. "Yes, I know of foreign ways, and Japan would benefit to learn of them too."

"How would that be possible?"

"It is obvious," she said.

"What, is obvious?" A soft male voice said.

Aiyana looked over and recognized the shogun. Up close he was smaller than she thought and bone-rattling thin, even under his loose purple robe. His hair was pulled back into a small knot, emphasizing protruding cheekbones. He looked to be about sixty years old. Aiyana stopped staring, she stood and bowed.

"Kenshin," the shogun said. "Why did you not tell me our guest had arrived?"

The councilor stood. "I was just on my way to summon you."

Aiyana could see the councilor, Kenshin, was lying through his crooked mouth.

"Hoshikosan," the shogun said, "please, sit, and tell me what you were about to say to Kenshin."

They took their places around a table. "What I was going to say, Shogun Ieyoshi, is that after being isolated for two hundred years, Japan would benefit by opening its borders to the world, not just the Dutch and a few others. You know, the Pacific Ocean it too big of a moat."

Kenshin's nostrils flared. "Sacrilege! Pay no mind to a woman."

Aiyana balled her fists. She knew she could take him out but was concerned about getting her head lopped off.

"Silence, Kenshin," the shogun said in an even voice.

A servant entered and placed a kettle of boiling water, bowl, whisk and tea powder on the table. He returned to serve green-tea soba rolled with cucumbers, shiitake mushrooms and mountain potato served on red lacquer ware. Without being told, Aiyana rearranged the dishes and started mixing the matcha tea and water.

"Hoshikosan, our country is thriving. Foreign powers are a threat to Japan, as you have seen. And Christianity undermines our feudal lords who rule the land."

Aiyana poured each of them a cup of tea. "I understand, Your Worship, but as you saw, the American ships in the harbor have the power to hurt a lot of people but they haven't. They just want you to peacefully sign a treaty. Captain Derek Blackburn is on shore and would like to meet with you to explain all the benefits of a settlement."

"Your danna?" the shogun said.

"Yes. And he trades with Japan so you can trust him. Can you please meet with him?"

The shogun drank some of his tea. "Perhaps I will. You seem to be very insightful, Hoshikosan. Is it because of your exotic blue eyes?"

Aiyana laughed. "Maybe."

The councilor's face reddened and a vein protruded at his temple. "Shogun Ieyoshi, I beg you, end this ridiculous conversation now."

The shogun raised a hand. "Kenshin, listen quietly or leave." He looked at Aiyana to continue.

"Shogun Ieyoshi, you can see the Americans aren't leaving. And I think you should know I had a dream of the future. If you don't agree to sign the treaty, the Americans will be back with more ships and cannons." She knew that overall the Japanese were a superstitious people so she had thrown in a psychic dream to add potency to her argument.

The shogun thought for a moment and nodded. "Kenshin, arrange a meeting with the American Commodore Perry in six days. Hoshikosan, return to my palace in seven.

CHAPTER 17

$\mathcal{T}$ime passed quickly on the carriage ride to Derek's cabin as thoughts of the palace visit played in Aiyana's head. This afternoon could have been classed as both a success and a failure. Successful for Commodore Perry, but a failure for her. She couldn't secure a meeting for Derek and that meant she wasn't going home. She sighed and for the first time in a long while, her energy was zapped.

She couldn't stop thinking about the pompous councilor's face, Kenshin, and how disrespectful he was to the shogun. And he seemed totally untrustworthy. She shuddered.

The driver helped her down from the carriage and she shuffled into the cabin. She sat at the table and unpinned her hair and it cascaded around her shoulders. While looking in the hand mirror she wiped off her make-up with a damp cloth. Derek's reflection appeared in the mirror.

He gently smiled. "I like your hair down."

Heat spread across her cheeks. How could such a simple statement make her feel so self-conscious? "I usually have it in a ponytail," she said and cringed. What kind of a response was that?

"How did your meeting go?"

Aiyana turned to face him. "Not as well as I hoped."

"The shogun didn't agree to meet with me did he?"

She put the mirror on the table. "No. Not yet. But he did agree to meet with Commodore Perry in six days. So, indirectly you'll be getting what you want. Right?" She held her breath and hoped he'd be appeased, but then she saw him frown.

He stepped forward and ran a hand along her hair. "It's not what I want at all."

His soft touch gave her shivers and she fought to focus on the issues on hand. "Derek, there may be one more chance for me to get you into the palace."

"When? How?"

"In seven days the shogun wants me back there."

"What does he want with you in seven days?" He pursed his lips.

"Maybe to discuss the treaty?"

"That, I seriously doubt. Forget it, Hoshikosan. I don't want you going there alone again."

She thought of the slithery Bakufu, Kenshin, and she agreed with Derek's sentiment. But, other than being exceedingly uncomfortable, she hadn't been in any danger. Perhaps the next time she went Kenshin wouldn't even be there. "Derek, I'm going. Don't worry; you know I can defend myself."

He smiled. "Oh, I know you can. But, if you are adamant about going I'm accompanying you."

"Okay, we can try that."

"It's decided then," he said. "Seven days." He had a far-away look.

"Derek?"

His attention shifted to her. "Yes?"

"It just looked like you were on another planet."

He moved closer and she inhaled his woodsy spice scent. He

then traced a hand lightly along her shoulder. "No, I'm here with you, on the same planet."

Goose shivers radiated from his touch. She had to focus and pulled away. "Derek, can you do me a favor?"

He raised his eyebrows. "What kind of favor?"

"After I get out of these clothes could you help me with my work out? The sparring part? I really like your moves, I mean, how differently you perform." She looked down, unable to meet his eyes which were probably sparkling with amusement. She fidgeted while waiting for his answer.

He let her squirm long enough. "Get out of those clothes, as you said, and I'll meet you outside."

The evening stars shone brightly and Derek was lighting lanterns. He blew out a lighted splint and noticed her. Her heart skipped at seeing him shirtless and in this romantic setting she wondered if she should have asked him to go one-on-one with her, so to speak.

Aiyana stretched and jogged on the spot and then they began sparring. Tentatively at first, then more heatedly. They challenged and adopted one another's techniques. A few times Aiyana landed on her back and stared up at the star studded sky. With a bruised ego, she was thrilled when she accomplished showing Derek the same view. After a lengthy session, Aiyana raised her hands, winded. "I can't believe this, but for the first time I think I've had enough."

"I like to keep my women satisfied." Sweat glistened on his bare chest and he flashed a gorgeous smile.

Aiyana wasn't used to kidding around with sexual connotation and her nervous laughter lasted longer than normal. "Well, I am very satisfied, Captain Blackburn. Thank you."

"Now *that* is a pity."

He took steps toward her and she stepped back. Her virginal flight response had kicked in. She dared to look up at him but he didn't seem annoyed, instead he smiled tenderly.

"So, Hoshikosan, we have six days to kill until all hell breaks loose on the beach."

Aiyana nodded.

"That's just enough time for my plans with you."

She widened her eyes. "What plans?"

"For that you will have to wait and see."

CHAPTER 18

*N*ot so long ago, choosing an outfit had never been difficult for Aiyana. Black or white cross-trainers? Gray or red sweats? But now, standing in front of a chest of impeccably folded kimonos, she found herself in a decision making dilemma. There was candy floss pink and sapphire blue. Both were lovely. Why was this so difficult?

Then it came to her. She wanted to look special for Derek. It was as simple as that. She got a tingling in her belly thinking about him. Often she asked for hints of where he was going to take her but he just smiled and said, "You'll see." He had instructed her not to wear pants so she suspected they wouldn't be visiting his ship.

She opened the second chest and on top was a pearly white kimono and obi. That was it. Decision made. White symbolized happiness and purity and this being like a first real date, she felt purely happy.

Mariko styled Aiyana's hair off her face and let it hang loosely down her back. At Aiyana's request, Mariko applied a more natural make-up with skin tone foundation and petal pink lips.

Aiyana was jittery from built up anticipation and took a deep breath to calm herself.

"The captain is waiting outside," Mariko said and handed her a parasol. "You are going to enjoy yourself very much."

Aiyana hugged her. "Thanks for all your help. Wait, do you know where we're going?"

Mariko pressed her lips together and raised her brows, appearing guilty as charged.

"You do know. And you're not talking," Aiyana said and laughed. "Sneaky girl."

Aiyana stepped onto the porch. Derek wore a white shirt, black pants and high black boots buffed to a shine. His green eyes darkened to a sultry hazel. They drank her in and set her heart racing.

He put out his arm. "Shall we?"

She slipped her arm in his and they strolled down the path to the carriage. She glanced sideways at Derek. "So, Captain, are you going to tell me where we're headed or are you going to keep me guessing?"

Derek's laughter resonated through the forest. "I was not going to divulge that information yet, so, my angelic Hoshikosan, I am afraid that you will have to keep guessing, as you had put it."

She shook her head and tried not to smile. "It's a conspiracy."

He chuckled and helped her into the open carriage parked on the dirt road. He hopped in beside her and when he flicked the reins the two blonde horses lurched forward. They rode to the sound of pounding hooves and the knocking and rattling of the wagon. The afternoon sun beat down on them and Aiyana opened the floral parasol and held it over their heads, making their ride more pleasant.

"Are we going to a sushi bar?"

"Sushi bar?"

"Yes. It's a restaurant for Japanese food."

He nodded. "There will be food where we are going."

"So it's not *just* a restaurant."

He glanced at her. "No, it is not."

"Theatre?"

Derek's mouth curled up one side.

"Hey, Captain sir, I don't like being in the dark."

"Dark? It's barely mid-day. And I'm afraid your impatience will not give you the answer you seek."

"Fine. I'll stop bugging you."

"Bugging?"

"Sorry about my vocabulary selection today. Where I come from, bugging means bothering or annoying."

"I see, but, your assumption is contrary to what I feel. I find your probing questions are most amusing, so, bug away."

She smiled. Once again he had made her feel special, and gave her a sense of safeness she had only felt with her father. She had been a white-uniformed student in a gym full of students, but because of her father, she knew she was different. He had said she had a unique fire and passion like no one else. And her mother. She supported in her own way by always standing by and quietly watching.

The galloping hooves gave off crisp clip-clops on the stone road they had turned on to. They had entered the city and Aiyana's attention was brought back to her present. People hustled on either side of the road. To her right she watched a barber walking along the road, holding the tools of his trade on the ends of a wooden stick slung across his shoulders. On one end was a small wooden bench and on the other a cylindrical container of his accessories. On the other side of the road were farmers who carried buckets of produce the same way on the ends of a stick. On a street corner, people crowded around a stone alter-like structure where an elderly woman sold chunks of bean curd.

Derek pointed ahead. "See that large building?"

A block away Aiyana saw a primitive, rustic looking dome. She nodded.

"That's where we are going."

She bit her bottom lip. Her excitement was growing the closer they got. They pulled over and Derek tied off the horses under the shade of a giant tree. She closed her parasol and left it under the bench. Derek then lifted her down and kept his hands on her waist. This time he wouldn't let her flight response kick in. She cleared her throat.

"So, the entrance is that way, Derek?"

He offered a bemused smile. "Yes, it is."

They entered the building through wide double barn-like doors into a massive arena. Stairs led up to several rows of bench seating. From the high ceiling hung huge black fabric scrolls with golden daisies, bordered by gleaming gold circles. But the main focus of the room was the center stage. Bales of rice-straw surrounded a circular clay ring. Derek had brought her to a sumo wrestling match!

She placed a hand on her chest as something tugged inside. "Derek, I'm speechless. Thank you."

He grinned. "You're welcome. Now come, let's get to our seats." He led her to benches three rows from the ring and waited for her to sit before he did. As the auditorium filled with eager watchers the murmurs of the crowd grew louder. Aiyana glanced around. There were very few females, and most of them were geisha as well. The anticipation in the air was as thick as the humidity and Aiyana couldn't contain her grin.

"Derek, do you have any idea what this means to me? This is Japan's national sport. Did you know sumo wrestling dates back to the sixth century?"

"Really? Then there must be merit to it."

She giggled at his formality. "Yes, there is merit to it and in mythology it is stated that sumo wrestling is popular with the gods."

"Well then, perhaps they will smile upon us as well."

The arena was bursting with spectators. Aiyana trembled. She felt electricity in the air. "I'm like a kid waiting for Santa," she said.

"Who?"

"I mean, St. Nicholas."

"You don't have to wait any longer. Look." He pointed to a slight man who started banging on an enormous gong.

A procession of enormous wrestlers paraded down an isle to center stage. Each wore silk shawl-like skirts and must have weighed between 250 to 400 pounds. The fans cheered at the contenders. The first two wrestlers remained at center stage while the others cleared out once again. Servants helped them undress to revealing girdles about their loins, covering only their privates.

The two rikishi, or wrestlers, stepped into the ring and began to loosen up. They raised one leg out to the side to waist height then heavily stomped down. Then they did the same with the other leg.

"See, Derek, that move is called shiko. It drives away stray devils."

Next, both rikishi scattered fists full of salt about the ring then rubbed some on their bodies.

Derek leaned over. "Why are they doing that?"

Aiyana answered without her focus leaving the ring. "Salt is a symbol of purity—it purifies the ring from the last bout's loss."

"Their philosophies almost make sense."

"Yes, they do. Look, they're starting."

The wrestlers stared at each other in a low squat, crouched like football linemen with fists touching the ground. With a word from the elaborately gowned referee, they slammed into each other, trying to heave the other to the floor or out of the fighting area. They crouched and yelled as they fought but as soon as one pushed the other out of the ring they both became quiet and courteous. The winner bowed to the loser and they stepped out of the ring. The crowd cheered and the next pair entered.

"It's over so fast, isn't it?" Aiyana said loudly.

Derek smiled and nodded.

"But, as fast as it is, there is so much skill and expertise involved. I could see it. And those bodies, they're huge but muscular. You can't get that way by eating just rice and tofu." Aiyana glanced at Derek who was still grinning at her.

Aiyana lifted her brows. "I'm rambling, aren't I?"

"Not at all. Your delight pleases me." He brushed his lips against her cheek. "You are different from every other woman I have known."

Nor had she ever met a man like him. He had enriched her life in every way. He proved to be a great match as a sparring partner, and now he captured her heart. She had to tell him and knowing their time together was limited she had to tell him now. She looked into his attentive eyes. "Derek—"

He pointed to the ring. "The next set is starting."

She exhaled. The moment of opportunity was temporarily lost. Hopefully there would be another.

Workers served trays of eggs, lobsters, oysters and cups of rice wine. Considering the venue, the meal was gourmet by any standard.

During the excitement of the match, Aiyana shifted in her seat and touched her thigh to Derek's. He probably hadn't noticed but she did, and she felt the heat. She wanted to get closer. Or perhaps it was the sake.

After several fights the show was over and the champion was awarded and applauded. Aiyana and Derek were in no hurry to file out and strolled casually to the carriage. Once again, Derek helped her up and she was disappointed this fabulous evening had come to an end.

Instead of turning the buggy around to go south to the coast, Derek steered it west. What was he up to now? Had he read her mind that she wasn't ready for this day to end?

"Derek? Where are we going now?"

He put the reins in one hand and pointed straight ahead with the other. Aiyana looked at lush forests, rolling hills and Mount Fuji with its white-capped peak.

"Wait, we're going to Mount Fuji?"

"Yes."

"But, it's so far."

He tipped his head. "It's far, but we have six days."

This sounded like fun in theory, but she was hardly prepared for a field trip. "But, I have no change of clothes, no food or a sleeping bag."

"Mariko packed everything we need."

Bless her helpful heart. Of course she knew where Aiyana was going, she helped pack.

"Are you sure we'll be back in time?"

"Absolutely. My whole mission here was to meet with the shogun, that is, until I saw you."

Aiyana lowered her gaze as warmth radiated within her. They continued riding along a dirt and gravel road under a canopy of trees. They came to a clearing on top of a hill. The descending sun cast radiating light over the forest and fields of the valley below.

Derek parked the buggy in a shelter of maple and cedar trees. "We'll make camp here for the night." He helped Aiyana down and carried a basket from the wagon over to a carpet of long grass. Next he tended to the horses while Aiyana spread out a pallet and couple of large gray blankets. She looked inside the basket and found a bottle of sake and two cups. She heard the soft rustle of Derek's approaching steps.

"Want a drink?" She asked Derek as he removed his boots and sat beside her.

"Yes, thank you." He accepted the cup and downed it in one shot. He crooked a brow at Aiyana. "You're not trying to get me drunk, are you?"

"Drunk?" Then she remembered the night she had posed the first challenge. He had known all along she had been trying to get him intoxicated. Damn. She couldn't pull anything over on this guy. "No, Captain, I'm not trying to get you drunk, but you don't get drunk, do you?"

He chuckled. "Not on this stuff. If I had a choice of spirit, it would be bourbon." He poured another cup. "What would you prefer to drink?"

Without hesitation Aiyana answered. "Evian." She looked down the gentle hill at the final fragments of sun touching the landscape.

"Hoshikosan, you're speaking in riddles again. Please enlighten me, what is Evian?"

"Oh, I'm sorry. It's bottled water from France. I drank it all the time back home."

"You've travelled to France?"

"Nope, just drank their water."

He looked at her then smoothed some hair off her forehead. His features were soft. "Somehow, I do believe there is truth in what you say."

Her heart swelled. She'd been wanting, needing to hear this all along. It was like he had taken a leap of faith and trusted her. "Derek, thank you for that, and for taking me to the tournament today. It meant the world to me."

"I know," he said softy.

"How could you know? You could have guessed or assumed but how could you know?"

He moved closer. "Because I love you." He kissed her lightly on the lips then trailed kisses along her cheek to her neck. She closed her eyes. He had said he believed her and loved her. He removed her hairclips and let her hair fall freely around her face.

He moved closer and his kisses deepened, he gave more and took more. His hands moved to her obi and she felt the confining fabric loosen and fall away. She didn't want to run anymore.

Her kimono opened and he trailed his mouth down her neck to her bare shoulders. She floated in wonderful sensations and it took a moment to realize Derek had stopped kissing her and had pulled away.

She opened her eyes and saw him looking at her with dilated passion. His breathing was heavy as he waited for a signal from her to proceed or to stop. Derek Blackburn was a gentleman to the very core. His expression seemed almost painful and she couldn't bear it, partly because she was in pain too. She wanted him and somehow knew this was meant to be. She slipped the kimono off her shoulders—the pure white silk that could have served as a wedding gown. The stars and moon shone from above and blessed them. She wanted Derek as much as he wanted her and at this moment that was all that mattered.

She reached forward and tugged his shirt out of his pants and pulled it over his head. She didn't want to hurry a single move-ment because she wanted to savor every moment and every sensation with Derek. Her tentative fingers moved over his chest, shoulders and abdomen, and she moved forward to kiss where her hands had been. His muscles flinched and this encouraged her to boldly use her tongue, which then drew a groan from him.

"Hoshikosan," he whispered.

She pulled back slightly, enough to say, "Please, call me Aiyana."

He breathed her name, "Aiyana, Aiyana," over and over. His arms folded around her and he kissed her deeply. His hands moved to her camisole and pulled it over her head. She shivered from the cool night air, or was it from his eyes on her, she wasn't sure.

"You're so beautiful."

"So are you." She reached out and put her arms around him

119

and pulled his lips to hers once again. Their bodies touched, his skin was velvet and hot and she pressed closer. Kissing wasn't enough. She wanted more of him. Derek gently laid her back. He brushed his hand over the tip of one breast, then the other and she took in a quick breath. In a smooth movement he moved his mouth to her soft mounds. His lips and tongue worked on her hardened peaks, lovingly tasting, gently prodding. His hand caressed a trail down her abdomen to her last piece of clothing and then he peeled it away.

She was totally bare, exposed to Derek and the heavens above. His lips parted as his gaze lingered on her.

"You can't be real," she thought she heard him say.

He moved back from her and removed the rest of his clothing. His silhouette was statuesque and perfect. Like a god. He dropped down to lay beside her again and kissed her feverishly. He pulled her close and every possible inch of their bodies touched. His hand moved to her core area and she stiffened, being touched there for the first time. He stroked and swirled and she sunk heavily into the ground. Sensations of heat and pleasure increased exponentially and a moan escaped her lips. She arched toward him. An aching need was building and her thoughts were fuzzy to everything but Derek. Her heart raced. He moved over her and nestled between her thighs. She wrapped her legs around him and felt his hardness, pulsating and pressing against her. He paused and her eyes fluttered open, heavy with passion. He had brought her to a point where it was cruel to stop.

"Derek, please."

In a swift movement he filled her. She gripped his shoulders and inhaled sharply at the split second of pain which soon ebbed. Derek started moving and intense pleasure mounted with each thrust. She clung to him, arched and moved with his rhythm. He filled her with every movement, deeper, faster. Her pleasure rose to a crest then exploded, holding her suspended. And then she felt his body shudder. His skin was damp and so was hers. With a final kiss he moved to her side and pulled her into his arms.

He cradled her closely and her body felt limp and fulfilled. She closed her eyes and the last thing she remembered thinking before she fell asleep was that she loved Captain Derek Blackburn.

CHAPTER 19

*A*iyana shifted lazily and awakened to the persistent chirping of birds. The pallet she lay on provided little cushion to the hard earth but she felt deliciously comfortable wrapped in thick wool blankets. The cool fresh morning air brushed over her face and she took a deep breath. Even though her body was limp she managed to stretch her heavy arm out to her side but found the space vacant. Sobered, she propped up on an elbow to search for the man with whom she had shared her whole body and soul the night before.

Aiyana heard a horse's whinny and looked in that direction. She smiled while watching him tend to the horses. Memories of last night replayed perfectly in her mind. If she weren't laying here naked she would question if their intimate union had really happened. Now she knew why she hadn't wanted to date or give herself to anyone before. She had been waiting for Derek. She continued watching as he brushed the horses; when he noticed she was awake he smiled and waved to her.

Derek walked over through tall grass, carrying a satchel in each hand. The rising sun shone through the trees behind him and she shielded her eyes with one hand and held the blanket close with the other. He smiled at her as he kneeled. Her tummy flipped and suddenly a rush of modesty washed over her.

"Good morning, gorgeous."

All at once her self-consciousness disappeared. The rich tone of his voice soothed her. "Hello, there."

"Did you sleep well?" he said.

"I slept, when someone wasn't keeping me awake," she shot him a sly smile.

He chuckled. "Please accept my apologies, my dear lady."

She feigned deliberation. "Okay, I'll forgive you if you have food in that bag. And clothes."

"Then I'm in luck. Though, you do look fine the way you are."

"Derek!"

"All right, all right, I will not torment you any further." He handed her one of the bags. "Mariko packed these for you."

Aiyana took the bag, removed a set of casual clothes and immediately started dressing. Derek often glanced at her as he put out some rice patties, and fruit. But, not knowing if anyone was in the area, she dressed quickly without giving a peep show.

She ate hungrily and drank from Derek's canteen.

"Aiyana?"

She slowly moved the container from her mouth. "Yes." She loved hearing him say her real name.

"Last night, why didn't you tell me?"

She swallowed and put the lid back on the canteen. "Tell you what?"

He tilted his chin down and wrinkled his brow. "Why didn't you tell me you had never been with a man before?"

He had figured it out. She looked at him and shrugged her shoulders. "The subject didn't come up, I guess."

He reached out, took her hand and caressed it. The deep green pools of his eyes pulled her in.

"I'm glad it was me," he said.

Her insides melted and she nodded. "Me too."

Together they put away the food they hadn't consumed and rolled up the pallet and blanket.

"Aiyana, can you ride?"

"I've ridden before." She didn't want to add it was on a pony at a birthday party ten years ago.

"Good," he said. "We'll leave the wagon here and will travel on horseback the rest of the way."

She glanced at the grazing horses. One of them pawed the ground with a hoof. "Derek, with you, every day is an adventure."

They packed up the rest of their supplies and saddled the horses. He was about to help her mount the mare when he pulled her into his enveloping embrace. His warm lips covered hers and gave her a tender, lingering kiss.

"Aiyana, last night was pure enchantment," he said softly.

She reached her arms around his neck and pulled him closer, deepening the kiss. Sparks of desire ignited. Automatically she pressed her body into his and felt his hardening response.

Suddenly the mare stomped impatiently and sneezed.

"You know," Derek said breathing heavily, "she's right, we better be on our way." He gave her a final peck and boosted her up on the horse. Aiyana sat rigid and clutched the reins tightly as the horse moved. "Whoa, that a girl," she said nervously.

Derek mounted his horse and rode over to her. "Everything all right?"

"Yup, fine," she said with some uncertainty.

"Let's go," he said and nudged the horse with his heels.

She did the same and her horse lurched forward. She nearly slid off the saddle and gripped tightly with her thighs to stay on. They trotted side by side and soon Aiyana adapted to the horse's rhythm. She turned to Derek and gave him a giant smile.

"Race you to the woods," she said and spurred on her horse. The horses' hooves rumbled across the field. Her heart pounded and she let out a throaty laugh, feeling the speed and wind rushing in her face and hair. Derek caught up to her and they raced until they reached forest. When they slowed down Derek circled before her. The horse stomped and Derek pulled on the reins to control the feisty animal. He wore a tight expression and glared at her.

"Aiyana, don't do that again. You could have been thrown." Blond hair fell wildly onto his forehead and his eyebrows were drawn together.

Her short-lived joy evaporated when she saw how worried he looked and realized how reckless she had been. "You're right. I'm sorry."

His features softened. "I just wouldn't know what to do if anything happened to you. Come on, ride behind me while we go through the woods."

They entered the forest and immediately the temperature dropped several degrees. They plodded single file through tall trees and dense brush. Their proximity to each other made conversing difficult so they rode to the symphony of chirping birds. Every so often they passed through warm, bright columns of sunshine where trees had left unbridged gaps. She closed her eyes and breathed in damp, earthy scents and rocked with the motion of the horse's steps. She felt one with nature, at peace, and alive in the moment.

A while later they emerged from the forest. They overlooked a meadow, bubbling stream and rugged, beautiful landscape stretching out to Mount Fuji.

"Derek, doesn't this view just take your breath away?"

"It absolutely does," he said.

"It's no wonder it inspires so many poets and painters. But, nothing is like seeing all this in real life. No wonder it attracts so many tourists from all around the world."

He tilted his head. "In the future, tourists from all around the world come here?"

"Yes, they do."

"How many?"

"Millions."

He raised his eyebrows. "Millions? That's a lot of tourists. And how do they travel here?"

"Mostly by airplane." She winced while watching him try to comprehend what she was saying. "Airplanes are like ships with wings that travel across the sky."

He nodded. "Well, Aiyana, I would very much like to see an airplane, and maybe even ride in one."

"Thanks for trying to believe me. I can only imagine how alien this all sounds to you."

"Oh, I don't know. If the Japanese can believe in the stars and gods of their festivals, airplanes don't seem unrealistic."

Aiyana smiled. "What a great way of looking at it, Captain."

"Now, would you like to stop and rest the horses down there?"

"Yes, and rest my butt too."

They nudged the horses down the hill. "Your butt?" Derek said. "I am assuming since you are sitting on a horse that refers to your behind."

"You assume correctly, Cap-ee-ton."

They stopped at the stream, took the saddlebags off the horses and then let the animals drink and graze. Derek spread out a blanket and removed his boots while Aiyana looked inside the lunch bag and pulled out food items one at a time.

"We have rice and veggies rolled in seaweed, some kind of fried dumpling and Asian pears."

Aiyana ate enough to satiate her hunger. She stretched and then dropped back and watched the clouds. In this instant everything was perfect. But what would happen in six days? Would she ever see her mother and Peter again?

Derek leaned on an elbow and watched her. "Are you in pain, Aiyana? Do you regret, anything?"

Beard stubble made him look more rugged and sexy, if that was at all possible, but it was his caring words that turned her on the most. She caressed his cheek then pulled his head down. Their lips merged in a tender, succulent kiss. Heat and desire wicked through her body and she felt like she was floating with the clouds. She moved closer and began undoing his belt. He placed a hand over hers.

"Aiyana," he said softly. "We've still got a lot of terrain to cover. You can't miss your appointment with the shogun."

Her senses crashed back to earth. "Shogun, right." She got up, packed their supplies and trudged to her horse without a backwards glance. He followed and helped her mount.

Why was she so upset? Perhaps it was because she realized she had fallen hopelessly in love and Derek didn't feel the same way. She thought he did, right up to the part where he prioritized business before her.

CHAPTER 20

erek and Aiyana rode at a steady pace for most of the afternoon. They didn't do a lot of talking, but she did do a lot of thinking. Summed up, her whole life's dream sat in the hand of a man she had come to love—she had no control over whether or not he would squeeze a fist, or open and release. The question that hovered in Aiyana's mind was, did she really want him to let her go?

From the corner of her eye she could see Derek looking at her. With her emotions swirling so close to the surface she couldn't bear to look in the eyes that took away all her reason. She leaned forward and patted the smooth fur on the mare's neck. Derek veered his horse close to her and she had to acknowledge him.

"Aiyana, I know I've said this before, but when I leave Japan I want you to come with me."

There they were. Passionate green-brown lasers that bore into her heart. "Derek —"

"You don't have to say anything now. Just, think about it."

She let out a breath and tried to release the squeezing pressure inside. Yes, it was best not to say anything right now because she wouldn't know what *to* say. Neither decision would result without heartbreak. For now, she had to let go of her incessant thoughts. She still had a few days with Derek, and she'd live them without any overshadowing emotions.

They entered a clearing and rode down a dirt lane into a small farming village. Modest homes were spaced apart on large plots of land. People worked around their homes and in the fields. They came upon a larger, pagoda style building that Aiyana realized was a temple.

"Derek, do you mind if we stop? I want to go in."

She slid off her horse and waited for Derek to do the same. But he remained mounted, making no effort to join her.

"Aren't you coming?"

"I shall wait for you here," he said.

"But don't you want to see inside?"

Derek gave a subtle shake of his head. A large cloud passed over, adding another hue to his darkened expression. He looked up then back at her. "Let's just say I'm not at peace with the almighty."

Turbulent emotions had to be brewing inside of him. And since they involved God, she knew he must have some serious issues to settle. "If you ask me, this would be a good place to start searching for some peace."

Derek's horse stomped impatiently but he remained seated. It was obvious he wouldn't be joining her. She turned and crossed the road toward the temple without him. Her steps slowed as she admired the smooth wood grain of the building. She slid open the door just as the sun broke free of the dark cloud and shone beams inside. She removed her dusty shoes and stepped inside.

She took quiet steps while looking around. The wood floor gleamed with a waxen finish and spicy incense permeated the air. On an altar, a Buddha faced her, round-bellied and sitting contentedly. Suddenly she felt uneasy. She didn't belong here, not without her father. This was a place they had wanted to see together and now that she was here she didn't desire to see it alone. Somehow Aiyana felt she would find solace in a Japanese temple but there was none of that, only feelings of grief, uprooted and amplified. Her chest felt tight and she needed air.

Aiyana backed up while eying the Buddha. *Maybe another time...*

She turned to sprint out and rammed full force into a solid chest, ricocheted off and fell back. Half dazed she looked up at Derek. "What the hell are you doing here?" She popped up and then stomped barefoot to get her shoes.

He loomed over her as she pulled them on. "I may be wrong, but is that appropriate language in this place?"

She straightened and scoffed at his amused expression. "Probably not, but do you really care? I mean, not being at peace and all?"

Swifter than a gust of wind, his expression darkened. "Woman, do not mock what you do not know." His voice was filled with a sadness she instinctively recognized because she had felt such pain herself. He went outside and she followed him to the horses.

"Derek, I'm sorry. I didn't mean to mock you, really."

In silence he helped her up on the horse and then mounted his. As they rode she frowned and quivered inside because her off-handed remark had hurt him. Why didn't she think before she said something so stupid?

"Please forgive me, Derek. Go ahead and mock me back. Go ahead. I'm ready."

He shook his head and half smiled. "I'm not mocking you back, Aiyana," he said and looked into the distance. "We must be getting close. I've heard about this place and wanted to see it before I set sail."

"It sounds like you don't plan on coming back."

Derek creased his brow. "Once I conclude my business I have no desire to set foot on Japanese soil again."

She tilted her head to the side. "That sounds so final. Why?"

His expression relaxed. "Once I take you with me there will be no need to return."

"That's a nice answer, Derek, but I get the feeling there is something you're not telling me."

He didn't confirm or deny her statement; instead he focused on the route through the dense underbrush. She decided the best thing to do was change the topic. "So, Derek, what made you decide to become a sailor?"

He narrowed his eyes. "Haven't you asked me that before?"

"Yes, but I'm still waiting for the rest of your answer. Tell me what inspired you to be a navy man."

"I'd rather talk about you."

Derek was being coy and Aiyana didn't have the patience to play his evasive game. She nudged her heels and the horse bolted forward and thundered through the woods. She gasped when she saw low tree branches and quickly ducked beneath them. Then her horse took flight and hurdled over a fallen tree. She leaned forward and squeezed her thighs to hold on for dear life. Adrenaline pulsed through her veins though she realized what she had done was loco.

Derek's horse rumbled behind. "Aiyana! Stop!"

She pulled on the reins to slow the mare down and glanced behind at Derek rushing to catch up. Suddenly there was movement in the woods beside her and her horse reared up on its hind legs. In a flash Aiyana was flying through the air. She landed with a thump and as she tried to orientate herself she realized a foot was still in the stirrup. Her horse stomped, ready to bolt again and Aiyana frantically tried to unhook her foot. Swiftly, Derek rode up, jumped off his horse and grabbed her mare's reins. He rubbed the length of the animal's nose to calm her and when she seemed placid he unhooked Aiyana's foot.

He dropped to his knees beside Aiyana with deep worry lines etched in his forehead. She sat shaking in a patch of coarse thicket, with blood dripping from abrasions on her hands and arms.

"Are you mad, woman?" His angry voice was laced with concern.

She nodded. "I must be." Her lips quivered and tears collected in her eyes.

He examined her cuts and grabbed a cloth and flask from the saddlebags.

"Thank you," she said and clenched her teeth from the stinging pain.

"Come on, let's get you up. Can you walk?"

"I think so." He helped her stand and looked deeply into her eyes. She was waiting for him to kiss her but it looked like he was struggling not to.

"We better get going," he said. "And this time you're riding with me."

≈

"You know, Derek, this isn't really necessary," Aiyana said while sitting in front of him on his stallion. Her horse was tethered to his and walked a short distance beside them.

"Oh I believe it is absolutely necessary. You could have broken your neck."

"I promise not to do it again."

"No good. I've heard that before," he said as they emerged from the forest.

They entered a meadow and on the other side of a wall of evergreen trees was the majestic Mount Fuji. Her heart thumped with excitement. "We're really close," she said and let herself ease back into him. He put an arm around her and his firm body cradled her cozier than a bean bag chair. The rocking motion of the horse and the cadence of Derek's breathing lulled her into a state of calmness, for the moment anyway.

"The reason I became a sailor was because of my older brother, William," Derek said.

She froze and sharpened her hearing, elated he was opening up to her.

"William was already first mate of an American ship when I was only ten years old. He was almost always away and being an orphan, I missed him terribly. I knew the only way to reach him was to become a sailor myself. As a sailor, I could go anywhere and nothing or no one would be too far—the world could be my port."

"And now it is."

"By the time I was eighteen I had become a captain in the same fleet as my brother. We went on many grand adventures together."

She could hear the pride in his voice. "Derek, where is your brother now?"

"Dead."

She squeezed her eyes shut and her stomach sunk. She had been afraid of this answer but had sensed it all along. She didn't know if she should probe him with any further questions, but then he started talking again.

"It was four years ago when William headed our fleet into Edo bay. A rowboat full of men went ashore; naturally William was one of them. We had come in peace and needed supplies, but the Japanese attacked us as soon as we stepped on dry land. Several were murdered immediately and the rest were taken hostage, tortured before they were killed. We could do nothing but stay on our ships, unless we wanted the same fate. They wouldn't even let us replenish our much needed supplies."

She put her hand on his. "Thank God you weren't one of them."

"For years I wished I had been. I was dead inside until one night I had a vision."

"A vision of what?" She wondered and felt warm breath caress her ear.

"Of you," he said softly.

Her heart skipped a beat, maybe two. She had been his vision? How was that possible? His story sounded almost as outlandish as hers.

"My mission had presented itself. So I signed on with a Dutch fleet and returned every year for four years to attempt to meet with the shogun, and, to find you."

Was that why she had somehow travelled back in time and felt such an irresistible attraction to him? Were they destined to be together?

She turned back to look at him. His lips parted and covered hers. His kiss was soft, loving. She pulled away slightly and traced small kisses along his cheek. "Derek, thank you for telling me everything."

CHAPTER 21

*T*o give his steed a break from the added weight, Derek reluctantly agreed to let Aiyana ride her own horse again. They emerged through a range of pine and cedar trees and stopped. Thick, lush vegetation carpeted the way to a graceful expanse of hundreds of fine waterfalls with Mount Fuji looming behind.

Aiyana's eyes widened. "Derek, the falls, they're breath-taking. And Mount Fuji is so much bigger than I imagined."

He shook his head. "Truly spectacular. Shall we get closer?"

"Yes, we shall."

The sound of rushing water got louder as they headed to a curved part of the falls plunging into a dark blue pool. They dismounted and Aiyana immediately removed her shoes and stripped to her underclothes. Smooth flat rocks lined the shore and could be seen in the shallow water with transparent clarity. She got her feet wet and then jumped back. "It's so cold," she said and looked over at Derek.

He smiled and began undressing. "It's only because you're so hot. I know I am."

His pecs bounced as he threw his shirt aside. "Oh, I know you are," she said, stroking her throat.

Derek joined her, and hand in hand they waded in.

He laughed out loud when they were waist deep. "It is quite brisk, isn't it?"

She stiffened in the frigid water and took quick breaths. "I think I'm numb from the waist down."

He crooked an eyebrow and pulled her into his arms. His mouth found hers and he kissed her deeply, with more familiarity. Having her eyes closed amplified other senses. She became even more aware of the touch of his smooth lips and the taste of his tongue, the smell of the fresh, crisp air and the sound of the pounding waterfall. He pulled back slightly and lightly rubbed his face against hers.

"I'm warming up," she said breathlessly.

He gazed at her with heavy lids. "Come," he said and guided her to the fine curtain of the waterfall and before she could protest he steered her through it. She shivered from the arctic splash and then looked around behind the falls in awe. He helped her step up into an alcove between the curtain of water and a wall of bedrock, weeping with moss and other foliage.

She slowly shook her head. "Just when I thought nothing could be more beautiful…"

He didn't give her a chance to finish. He continued the kiss he started earlier, but with more fervor and urgency. His mouth moved over her face and neck, not leaving an area untouched. He pulled off the remnants of her clothes and then removed his. Her nipples were already beaded and ready for his touch; his hands kneaded and teased. He dropped to a knee and placed his mouth on a breast. He circled his tongue and lapped her in, first one side, then the other. She ran her fingers through his hair as he created sensations she never knew were possible. The nucleus of her womanhood ignited and need intensified. As if sensing her aching desire, Derek trailed his way down. His tongue moved to the core of her and her knees weakened. She took air in ragged gasps and the rising pleasure drove her mindless. In a swift movement he stood and effortlessly lifted her, cradling her while she straddled him. A blunt hardness pressed, but went no further. She opened her eyes. His lips were parted as he looked at her with widened pupils. His body trembled.

"I can't lose you," he said and tipped his head.

A seam ripped along Aiyana's heart. He was tormented and she didn't know what to say to comfort him. Right now she could only show him.

"Make love to me, Derek," she said and wrapped her arms around his neck. Suddenly his thickness filled her and she drew in a rapid breath, not in pain, but from deep, penetrating pleasure. He moved and with every stroke the pleasure increased but so did the aching need for release. She heard the sound of the rushing water vaguely in the distance as Derek drove her to the point of insanity. In a flash, her orgasm exploded and shook her in waves which slowly receded and left her drained. Gently he put her on her feet and held her close. She listened to the deep drumming in his chest as it slowed and in their afterglow her eyes filled with tears. A lifetime wouldn't be enough with Derek, let alone these few days. But which one would it be? He had just shown her he had no intention of letting her go, and in these tender moments, she didn't want him to.

CHAPTER 22

On the final night of their journey home, Aiyana and Derek hunkered down in an area of soft grass near a cluster of stunted fir bushes. On a sandy patch of earth they fashioned a ring of rocks, gathered wood and kindling and lit a fire. While watching the crackling flames Aiyana sat snuggled in Derek's arms and basked in how secure and cared for he made her feel. He stroked her hair.

"Aiyana?"

"Yes?" she said softly, hearing weariness in her own voice.

"Tell me about your family."

She felt warmth and adoration at his caring question and put a hand over his. But his question also touched emotional strands inside and she teetered towards tears yet again. "Back home it's just my mom and me. But, we're not on the best of terms right now. I have a really good friend though, Peter, who's like a brother."

"What of your father?"

She zoned in on the orange flames. "He passed away when I was eleven, here in Japan, during a tournament."

He pulled her closer. "The tournament you want to get

back to."

Her throat tightened and she nodded.

"And that is why you and your mother are at odds," he said softly.

"Pretty much," she said, impressed he had assessed her situation so easily. "I don't think my mother ever really understood the whole martial arts thing, and she should have, having a husband and daughter so involved in it. You know, deep down, I think she was envious of all the time my dad and I spent together at the gym." Fragmented memories of her father flashed through her mind and tears burned her eyes and then spilled. Almost all the memories of her father were tied to the gym and her soul connected to her father whenever she used the skills he had taught her. She shook as she inhaled. Derek stroked her hair again and she closed her eyes. Her body was sinking and succumbing to exhaustion. "I have to win prize money to keep the gym open. If I don't, I'll lose my dad all over again," she said in a whisper before falling asleep.

The next morning dark billowy clouds moved overhead. They quickly packed up camp and had a hard ride through almost impenetrable masses of brush wood and dense foliage. The horses plodded slowly with high steps through the coarse herbage.

He wiped sweat off his brow. "Sorry I took this route, Aiyana, I thought this one would have been faster."

"Don't worry about it, but when we get back, make sure to give the horses an extra bucket of oats."

He smiled. "That I will."

He looked up at the dark and foreboding sky that cast a dark eeriness over the land. "I hope the rain holds out a while longer," he said. "The last thing we need are bolts of lightning."

By mid-day they got back to the wagon and hitched the horses to it. Aiyana stretched and welcomed the change of position. The wind had cooled and picked up substantially and as they turned onto a road thunder rumbled in the distance. Derek pushed the horses as hard as he could without exhausting them when all of a sudden lightning flashed and the heavens opened. Water streamed down on them for the rest of the journey. When they arrived at the cabin, Derek helped her down. The storm picked up its intensity. The rain poured and the wind whipped.

"You go inside, I'll finish up here!" Derek said.

She nodded then started running in but stopped to glance back. He unhitched the wagon from the horses. His clothes were plastered against his body as he worked, hopping over puddles as he moved around.

As she watched she became aware of the strong pounding of her own heartbeat. Lord he was attractive. And he had no idea of how much she desired him right now.

"Hoshikosan!" Mariko waved from the porch. "Come now!"

Aiyana turned and ran up the stairs. "Mariko, it's so good to see you." They went inside and Aiyana changed her clothes and towel-blotted her hair. She joined Mariko at the fire pit, stirring a cauldron of wonton soup with a wooden ladle.

The savory aroma made Aiyana's mouth water and stomach grumble and she tried to muffle the sound with her hand. "Pardon, me," she said.

Mariko smiled. "Hoshikosan, two days ago another messenger from the palace came here."

Aiyana's hand moved to her chest. "What did they want?"

"They had another scroll to give to you but I said you weren't here and would be gone until today."

"Is the scroll here?"

She shook her head. "No, they wouldn't give it to me."

Aiyana tried to think of reasons the palace would send a message to her. She jumped when Derek burst through the door then forced it shut behind him. He shook his head and then peeled off his clothing to his under shorts.

"Oh, hello, ladies," he said.

Mariko lowered her eyes and excused herself to her bedroom. Aiyana smiled but didn't say anything about the girl's shyness. She scooped out soup for the both of them. "Here, Derek, this should hit the spot."

Scantily clad, he walked over with his wet skin glimmering. Aiyana gulped. He sat and accepted the bowl.

"Thank you," he said and together they slurped from their dishes. He ladled out another helping for himself and quickly ate that too. He smacked his lips. "That was good but I really miss red meat, buffalo or venison, hell, even a wild turkey would be nice."

She widened her eyes. "I was just thinking the same thing, except I'd settle for a hamburger and onion rings."

"Foods from the future?" he said and grinned.

"Yeah, they're great."

"One day I'd like to have a hamburger with you."

She nodded. "That would be nice," she said, but the thought was more than unlikely.

Derek yawned and rubbed his eyes. Aiyana took the bowl from his hands.

"I'll tidy up here, you go lay down. I'll be there in a minute."

His hazel eyes reflected light from the fire. He leaned toward her. "Don't be long," he said in a thick, mellow voice and left the room.

Aiyana tidied up the dishes and extinguished the flame in the cooking pit. The storm still pounded outside and she hoped a giant tree branch wouldn't crash down on the cabin. She tiptoed into the bedroom and saw Derek in bed, shirtless with the covers around his waist and watching her with an arm behind his head.

"You're not asleep yet?"

"No," he said with a serious demeanor. He pulled the covers

back for her and in doing so he revealed a bare thigh. She swallowed and turned to snuff the lantern's flame.

"Electricity, that's what I really miss." She glanced at him and his eyes drank her in. She couldn't decide if he was really listening to her but she continued anyway. "It's like having lanterns that are brighter, without the danger of fire."

She crawled into bed and he pulled her into his arms. She heard the soft rhythm of the rain and low rumbling of thunder in the distance. The worst of the storm was over, but for her, the worst was yet to come.

His breath caressed her cheek and he stroked her shoulder with feathery touches. She closed her eyes and revelled in being beside him but thoughts of the days to come started dominating her mind.

"So, are you looking forward to seeing Commodore Perry come ashore tomorrow?" she said.

"Perhaps. But tomorrow will just be shenanigans. It's the day after I'm waiting for."

"Seeing the shogun," she said quietly.

"Yes."

She sighed. As close as they were, physically and emotionally, he still had a thin, impenetrable casing she couldn't get through.

"Aiyana, I'm sure you have thought about whether or not I am willing to uphold our wager."

She opened her eyes and stared into the darkness, waiting for him to continue.

"I am a man of honor, and I will return your possession as promised, *if* I meet with the shogun. Although, every fibre of my being tells me to steal you away and keep you captive on my ship."

Aiyana turned to softly kiss his lips. Her gentle act was all that was needed to ignite their flaming passion once again.

But Derek, don't you know? You already hold me captive.

CHAPTER 23

*W*hen Aiyana awoke the next morning she noticed Derek was gone. She pulled on a robe and walked through an empty house. She went outside to search for Derek and Mariko. The storm had left a cloudless sky, fresher air and greener plants. Mariko was hanging clothes on a line.

"Good morning, Hoshikosan."

"Hi, Mariko. I hadn't realized I slept so late. Do you know where the captain is?"

"Yes, he went down there." Mariko pointed to the beach and Aiyana walked to the brow to look down. In the few days she and Derek were gone a structure had been built and it looked like the security detail had tripled. She had to go down there to see things for herself up close. She dared not miss Commodore Perry's entourage and the presentation ceremony.

She glanced on the clothes line and saw all her casual clothes hanging, sopping wet, which meant she had to wear a kimono to the beach.

"Mariko, I hate to bother you but can you help me dress?"

The girl put down her basket. "Yes, of course, Hoshikosan."

Inside, Mariko pinned up Aiyana's hair and she thought her friend deserved to know some truth about her.

"I want you to know I am grateful for all your tireless help. In this short time you have become a special friend to me and for that reason I want you to know my real name isn't Hoshikosan. It's Aiyana."

Mariko lowered her gaze. "I consider you a friend as well, Hosh--Aiyana."

"And, the reason I'm telling you this is because I will be leaving soon."

"You're leaving Mother and the house?"

Aiyana nodded. "And when I do leave, I want you to have all of my belongings."

Mariko opened her eyes until they were almost round. "But all of your kimonos are worth a fortune."

"You deserve them. You are a beautiful, kind girl." Aiyana turned and hugged her. In these recent days Aiyana's tears were constantly close to the rim. Aiyana sniffed and struggled to stop the impending flow. "Now, Mariko, please help me choose an outfit."

They agreed on a lilac kimono and sky blue obi. Mariko said she reminded her of a summer flower. Aiyana gave her a final hug before heading down the hill. With no one around to see her, Aiyana hiked up the gown for the trek to the beach and then she smoothed it back down when she got there.

The beach front had become more congested than an amusement park on a national holiday. While looking around for Derek, Aiyana weaved her way toward the large, hastily erected Audience Hall made of wood and cloth. It had giant columns, a gable roof with deep eaves and walls of fabric. She stiffened and warily glanced at lines of armed samurai guarding the structure. She managed to glance inside and saw a large table and several government officials standing about the room. The shogun stood out in a dark brown kimono with his hair knotted back and close to him in gray was the creepy bakufu councilor, Kenshin. He was looking toward the bay and then noticed her. They made eye contact and she cringed. She felt hands slip around her waist and reflexively she rammed back an elbow.

"Awe, Aiyana," Derek said in a tight voice.

Aiyana turned and placed her hands to his abdomen. "Derek, I'm so sorry, are you all right?"

"I'll survive," he said as he looked around. "Aiyana, I want you to go back to the cabin. The situation here is volatile."

The murmurs of the crowd heightened and Aiyana and Derek looked out to the bay. Several boats from Commodore Perry's fleet were rowing ashore. Swarms of samurai forced them back to allow a vacant beach front for the Americans. The boats pulled up on the sandy shore and sailors disembarked. The first to arrive were the marines, then officers and musicians. Like a tsunami, boatloads kept arriving.

Samurai patrolled the crowd border and then unexpectedly several Samurai circled around her and Derek.

"Hoshikosan," one of them said. "The shogun requires your presence in the Hall." A glint from the samurai's razor sharp sword indicated the topic wasn't up for discussion.

Aiyana looked up at Derek and his eyes narrowed warily. He placed a protective arm around her.

"Derek, I think this should be okay. They probably want me to translate."

He leaned toward her ear. "Just stay close to me," he said, casting iron glances around.

She stepped away from the crowd but the samurai blocked Derek. The escort forced her forward but she kept glancing back. Derek repeatedly pushed against a restraining line of warriors until a samurai unsheathed a sword and held it to his neck.

Her heart beat so hard it threatened to rip out of her chest. "Derek, stop!" she yelled, fearful of what would happen if he resisted any further. She tried to pull away from the guards but they held each arm strong and thrust her forward. The last glance of Derek was of him backing into the crowd, thankfully, alive.

They entered the towering Audience Hall and the samurai released Aiyana. Wearing a sneer, the councilor approached her. She shivered and felt hair prickle on the back of her neck.

"Hoshikosan, come, Shogun Ieyoshi is waiting." He crossed his arms and turned, expecting her to follow like a puppy, and having no choice in the matter she followed. They walked over to the table where the shogun stood. Aiyana bowed and he nodded in return.

"Hoshikosan, for days my officials have tried to locate you and now by heavenly intervention you are here," the shogun said in a feeble voice, his skin appeared thinner and more wrinkled since the last time she'd seen him.

She couldn't disagree—her whole experience here was by some kind of unearthly intervention. She bowed again. "Shogun Ieyoshi, what is my purpose here?"

"You have knowledge of the Americans and speak both languages. You will act as a liaison."

She nodded. "I can do that." Fully realizing her role in the unfolding events made her tremble and she took a deep breath to steady herself. She thought of Derek.

"Shogun Ieyoshi, may I request my danna accompany me during this task? He could also be of assistance."

Kenshin turned to the shogun who seemed to be considering her request. "Your Excellency, I would strongly advise against it. He's a foreigner and you know they can't be trusted."

Aiyana started to protest but the councilor raised a delicate hand to silence her. She had to stop herself from grabbing and twisting it behind his back to drop him to his knees.

All of a sudden the musicians played and everyone's attention was drawn to the shore—Aiyana took steps forward to get a better look.

Commodore Perry's boat was the last one to arrive and he

stepped onto the sandy shore. He and his entourage of some three-hundred men marched past armed samurai toward the Hall. She held her breath and when all seemed to be unfolding without incident she breathed again. When she saw Commodore Perry walking toward them in his high-collared navy uniform with shiny brass buttons her breath caught again. He held his chin level and back straight as he entered the Hall. He removed his hat to reveal brown hair combed to the side. He wore an even, impassive expression and stopped in front of the shogun.

"Shogun Ieyoshi, I am Commodore Matthew Perry from the United States of America. Thank you for granting permission to step onto your shores," he said in a strong, authoritative voice.

The shogun glanced at Aiyana and she stepped forward.

"Commodore Perry, my name is Aiyana Amari," she said and cleared her throat. "May I say it is an honor to meet the man who will change the course of history between the East and the West?" She bowed.

His lips curled into a kind smile and he nodded once. "And may I say it is lovely meeting you too, Miss Aiyana. I must say your English is impeccable."

"Thank you, sir, my mother is American."

The councilor stepped closer and his nostrils flared. "Hoshikosan, translate."

She turned to the shogun and explained what the commodore had said. The shogun bowed and the commodore mirrored him.

Commodore Perry turned to his lieutenant who handed him the official narrative of the Perry mission, the commodore then placed it on the table in front of the shogun. "This is a letter from President Fillmore. It explains that we seek peace and prosperity for both countries."

Aiyana conveyed what Commodore Perry had said. Then the commodore requested good treatment of castaways, the allowance of Japan to be a refueling station for ships, and to grant the acceptance of an American consul.

Aiyana translated as completely as she could and both men seemed willing to listen and negotiate.

At the end of the meeting the commodore leaned toward the shogun, and even though there was a language barrier he spoke directly to him none-the-less.

"Shogun Ieyoshi, I will return shortly for your answer with a larger squadron, more ships and more fire power."

Aiyana explained the impending situation to the shogun. In conclusion of their business, the two men nodded to each other and the commodore turned to leave. He looked at Aiyana, picked up her hand and kissed the back of it.

"Thank you, my dear, for your service. Please ensure the shogun understands the ramifications if he refuses."

Aiyana bowed. "I will, Master Commodore. And have a safe voyage," she said.

He smiled at her and turned to lead the procession to the shore. Murmurs from the watching crowd grew louder and Aiyana scanned the swarm of people for Derek and hoped he had somehow seen the proceedings. The Japanese officials were escorted by samurai guards and Aiyana was grouped in with them. She tried to leave but they wouldn't let her weasel out. She caught up to the shogun.

"Excuse me, Shogun Ieyoshi, may I go home now?"

"No."

"No, why? I've done what you've asked and I'd like to get home for my danna," she said.

The shogun stopped. "Now you belong to me," he said. "I am your new danna."

CHAPTER 24

A procession of covered carriages carrying the government officials rolled back to the palace. Aiyana sat stiffly in the same coach as the shogun and the unnerving bakufu, Kenshin. She repeatedly looked out the window hoping for the unlikely chance to see Derek riding beside her. Where had he gone after the samurai had forced him back on the beach? Did he return to the cabin or perhaps his ship? Did he even know she was gone? She let out a breath and wiped perspiration off her forehead. Her situation had become worse than she could have ever imagined. The shogun had become her danna? How was she ever going to get home?

The two men across from her stared at her and she swallowed sourness rising in her throat. Maybe she'd try to reason with them.

"Shogun Ieyoshi, I request to be released at once. I am resigning as a geisha."

The shogun grimaced and she didn't know if he was thinking or passing gas. "Resigning? I was not made aware of this. Hoshikosan, as far as I understand, I am your danna for the next year. A large purse was settled for you."

She clenched her jaw and was getting tired of being bought and paid for. Kenshin remained silent and ran fingers over his mouth. Once again hairs rose on Aiyana's neck.

"Shogun Ieyoshi," she said, trying not to plead. "Will you please let me go if I return the money you paid? This is all a mistake. I do not wish to have any danna anymore."

The shogun pressed his lips tightly together and frowned. While waiting to hear his response Aiyana quickly glanced out the window, at Kenshin and then back at the shogun.

"Well, Hoshikosan," the shogun said, "if you are unwilling, I will not force you. But, I insist you stay for dinner while my officials settle matters with the mother of your house."

A thousand pounds lifted off Aiyana's chest and she slowly smiled. "Thank you very much, Shogun Ieyoshi. If I may be so bold, do you by any chance know where Captain Derek Blackburn is? I haven't seen him since Commodore Perry arrived."

The shogun nodded. "Yes. He has been banished."

A sudden coldness hit the core of her. "But why?" she said. "I thought he was a welcome trader."

The shogun thought for a moment. "He is. But Kenshin advised me that Captain Blackburn has no more to trade at this time and if he lingers he may become a threat. With him gone, your services became available, or so I assumed."

She pinched her lips together in frustration and her heart beat hard. *Think Aiyana, think.*

The convoy turned onto the bridge leading to the palace and their carriage stopped at the main entrance. Ironically, the first time she was at these grounds was during the festival where she was scheming a way to get away from Derek, and now she was contriving a way to get back to him.

The carriage doors opened but before the shogun moved to exit she leaned forward. "Shogun Ieyoshi, can you please answer one more question?"

He tipped his head. "Yes, of course."

"You said Captain Blackburn is banished, what does that mean? I mean, when does he have to set sail by?"

The shogun feebly got up and turned before stepping out of the carriage. "He must be gone by sunrise."

She bit the inside of her cheek. Damn. That didn't give her much time at all. Next, Kenshin got out and told her to follow. Samurai stood on either side of her and she thought the security detail was a bit much. They entered through the familiar doorway into the foyer with parquet flooring and the ceiling of gold. The first time she was there Aiyana had stopped to admire the beauty. She wasn't in the mood today.

Kenshin guided her to the room on the left where samurai stood on either side of the entrance. She was told to wait for further instructions. The door slammed behind him and she jumped.

"Good riddance," she said. She glanced around at the wall murals and the low square oak table surrounded by cushions. She looked out the window and then paced the room. She stopped in front of the stone Buddha. He sat in a lotus position with his hands folded and his eyes closed.

"Easy for you to be relaxed, buddy." She talked to him like a real person and realized she was becoming unhinged.

It was mid-afternoon and the pressure was on to get out of here and find Derek. She had a finite amount of time trickling too fast in an hour glass. Some thirty minutes later a woman wearing a green and white checked kimono entered carrying a box and a basket. She bowed to Aiyana.

"Bakufu Kenshin requests you wear this for your portrait," she said without any hint of pleasantness.

Aiyana widened her eyes. "I have to change for a portrait? I thought I was just staying for dinner."

The woman ignored her and stepped forward to help her dress. One thing for certain, she was no Mariko. When the servant pulled the kimono out of the box Aiyana instantly realized it looked familiar. Silvery turquoise—the kimono from the souvenir shop. She felt dizzy as she got dressed. She didn't know what was real anymore. The kimono was as tight as a strait jacket, the woman painfully manipulated Aiyana's hair into an up-do, and then applied make-up on her face and neck. There was a knock on the door.

"Enter," the woman said and placed a chair by the window for Aiyana to sit on. She then backed out of the room.

A man in a loose beige tunic and pants entered carrying a roll of paper, wooden sticks, and a basket. He bowed and set up an easel with paper and laid out coal pencils on the table. He motioned for her to sit and she obliged. She watched his face as he worked. He squinted and moved like a jittery rabbit with short quick movements. Sitting here helpless was like being in a bad dream, no, worse, she was living an impenetrable nightmare.

She was given a break every now and then to stretch and each time she looked impatiently out the window. Thankfully he wasn't talkative because she didn't feel like conversing. The sun was almost down and her situation was becoming more dire by the second. Finally, after several excruciating hours he completed his drawing. As he packed up his equipment she went over to see what had taken so long to draw. She looked at it and recoiled. Her own blue eyes stared back at her. It was the portrait from the Temple Inn.

"Nuts," she whispered. "I really am her," she said in disbelief. Then she remembered the sad story about the drawing.

Rumors said Shogun Ieyoshi died after the exotic geisha left him. Her shaky knees threatened to buckle. Yes, she was going to leave the palace that part was true, but the shogun hadn't seemed sick about it. None of this made sense.

She hadn't noticed the artist was gone, only that Kenshin had entered and a servant followed. The servant put a tray of food on the table, lit the lantern and then left. She stood, frozen.

"Where is Shogun Ieyoshi? I was supposed to have dinner with him and then be on my way."

The man raised his brows and crinkled his long forehead. "Shogun Ieyoshi has retired. I am here in his stead. Now, sit, and eat."

The only reason Aiyana sat at the table was because of the need for sustenance. She sat and ate heaping mouthfuls of fish, rice and fruit. Kenshin didn't eat; he just rubbed the few whiskers on his upper lip and stared at her. She couldn't bear to look at him so she glanced at the window. It was dark and her time was running out.

"Well, Mister Kenshin, thank you for dinner and now I will be on my way."

He shook his head on his scrawny neck. "I'm afraid you won't," he said.

Heat flooded her face. "But I'm allowed to go. The shogun said so."

"But I am saying you are not."

She jumped up and nearly tipped over in the tight kimono. She took tiny steps to the door. "I demand to see Shogun Ieyoshi." She opened the door and the two samurai warriors banded together to block her way. She immediately shut the door.

"Why are you keeping me here? You have no right."

"There you are wrong, Hoshikosan, I have every right, because now you belong to me."

"Like hell I do," she said and wanted to spit.

He gave a snively laugh. "You see, the shogun's actions were pathetic today. He was spineless and showed no force to the Americans, or to you. I, on the other hand, am forceful."

He stepped before her and she made no effort to hide her distain. "You are mad."

"Not at all. Rulers should have my qualities. Influential, dynamic, ruthless."

Whenever she saw this guy her instincts screamed to get away from him and now she knew they were bang on. She needed to get to the shogun to tell him his bakufu was a treasonous pig. He reached out to touch her cheek with a scrawny finger and she slapped his hand away.

"Is that how you acted with your Captain Blackburn? Or did you writhe for his touch?" He shot out an arm and ripped open her kimono. He lunged forward and squeezed her to him with surprising strength. He groped as if he had four hands. Her mind reeled at the assault and her body exploded with adrenaline. She stomped on his foot, twisted out of his grip and smacked him in the nose with an open palm. He stepped back and dabbed blood from his arrogant nostrils.

He nodded. "For that, your captain's head will be on a spike."

Upon hearing Derek was in danger she froze. What could she do to save him? This guy couldn't be reasoned with—she had to escape, get to his ship and warn Derek. She ran to the window and tried to open it. Kenshin grabbed her from behind. She placed a foot on the wall and pushed, propelling them back. They landed with a thud. She scrambled away from him and just as she stood to run he grabbed her kimono. She dropped forward like a falling tree and cracked her skull on the stone Buddha.

Pain speared through her head and her mind became foggy. She was vaguely aware her kimono was being ripped open and she felt hands molesting her thighs. He pulled back for a moment and she crawled away but he was on her again in a second. When he kissed her she bit him and then he put a pillow over her face. She fought wildly for air and managed to toss the pillow away. It hurled across the table and sent the lantern flying. Instantly flames ignited the lamp oil trail and engulfed the table and cushions. Soon the room was raging with fire and smoke.

She couldn't move, her body was as heavy as lead. Smoke burned a searing path from the back of her mouth into her lungs and she didn't have the strength to cough, only gasp. She was losing consciousness and had no choice but to accept that this was the end.

In the distance she heard broken glass, a concussive bang and then felt arms lift and carry her. She tried opening her eyes but they burned and teared. She sensed cool fresh air which kept her from drifting away.

Someone was calling her name from the end of a long tunnel. A hand brushed over her temple and she managed to open her eyes but she didn't have to see to know that she was in Derek's arms.

"Aiyana." He pulled her closer. "Thank God. Are you all right?"

She squeezed a handful of his shirt. "Derek," she said almost inaudibly. "You're in danger." She caught a glimpse of something shiny in his hand before he moved it away.

"Shhh. Don't worry about me love. Let's get you out of here."

CHAPTER 25

*A*iyana jerked awake and stared into the shadows. Sweat covered her brow and she tried to stifle a cough through a sore throat. She was alone in bed and sat up. Derek was sitting on a chair and then dropped to her side. He softly stroked hair away from her face and touched a tender area on her temple.

"Ahh." She lifted her hand and felt a goose egg. Her heart started pounding as she remembered what happened in the palace. "Derek," she said in a raspy voice. "We shouldn't be here. The bakufu—he's probably going to kill both of us."

Derek shook his head. "No, he won't." He reached for a cup on the bedside table. "Drink this, Aiyana. It's ginseng, honey and some other root. Mariko said this would heal your throat and help with the pain."

She took a few sips and the tea soothed on its way down. "It's good," she said and drank the rest. She had to convince Derek how desperate their situation was. "Derek, your head, and mine, will be put on a stick. Palace guards are probably on their way." She tried to get up but he gently put a hand on her shoulder to stop her.

"Aiyana, what do you remember from yesterday?"

"Well, the shogun took me to the palace, he was going to have dinner with me but didn't show up, only the creepy bakufu Kenshin did." Detailed memories rushed back. "Kenshin said you were banished and he was my new danna. He attacked me and I hit my head. And I knocked over a lantern." She widened her eyes. "The palace?"

Derek nodded. "It's in flames. No one is coming from there."

After hitting her head and laying barely conscious in a smoke-filled room, Aiyana remembered the sound of smashing glass and a bang.

"Derek?"

"Yes?" He said as he wrung out a facecloth and placed it on her forehead.

"You saved my life. Thank you." Her heart felt full of love, adoration and gratitude.

He placed her hand in his. "A feat I'd do again and again."

She smiled and let sleep overtake her. No one ever talked like that anymore.

Derek hadn't left her side all night; it was only in the morning she noticed him standing by the window. She squinted at the brightness and sat up. She was surprised at how good she felt. The pain in her head, chest and throat had become a mere discomfort. She stood and joined him at the window and stared out into the forest.

"Good morning," she said and wrapped an arm around him. He did the same. "Derek, hey, you seem a million miles away."

He pulled her closer.

Her thoughts had more clarity and a few holes presented themselves from last night's story. "Derek? What were you doing at the palace last night? How did you know I was there?"

"I was wondering when you'd be asking that. I saw you leave

the beach with the shogun and followed the procession to the palace."

She turned to face him. "After I smashed my head, did I imagine hearing a gun shot?"

He pressed his lips together. "No, you didn't."

"What were you doing there with a gun, Derek?" She thought for a minute and the pieces connected. Her eyes widened. "Of course, how didn't I figure this out sooner? It's the reason you came to Japan. You didn't want to negotiate trade and free ports with the shogun like Commodore Perry had. With you it was more personal than that, wasn't it?"

He stood vey still. "I had to avenge my brother's death."

She stepped back. "Did you murder the shogun?"

"The shogun is dead. Slain in his quarters."

She put a hand to her mouth.

"He is dead," Derek continued, "but not by my hand."

"What? Then by who?" She thought of the man who had openly showed distain for the shogun and called him spineless. "Kenshin," she said. It all made sense now. That was why the shogun hadn't joined her for dinner. He was already dead. And with the shogun out of the way, the councilor claimed her for himself. She shivered.

"The bakufu?"

Derek nodded. "Now he I did kill. I wish I could have many times over for his harming you."

"Is it true they banished you?"

"Yes. The distraction of the fire gave us more time to prepare but the ship and crew are ready. We set sail today."

The wind whooshed out of her lungs. Derek was leaving Japan. This day of resolution had actually arrived and she would find out in which direction her fate would take her. "Derek, technically I failed to arrange a meeting."

"No, it is I who failed you." He clenched his jaw and she looked into his tormented eyes.

"What are you talking about, Derek? If you had failed me I wouldn't be here, alive and talking."

He shook his head. "No. It was because of me that you were in grave peril and it is I who must apologize to you. I should have never made that wager with you but I was so hell-bent on revenge and filled with rage. Because of my idiocy I almost lost you. Please accept my deepest and most humble apology."

She stroked his cheek. "Derek, you couldn't see into the future so who would have expected there to be a fire. Anyway, it was all for nothing. I couldn't get what you wanted."

"You're the one I want. You are all that matters." He wrapped his arms around her waist. "Sail with me," he breathed. "Leave Japan with me. I am in love with you and my love runs deeper than any ocean. When I think that I almost lost you I practically go out of my mind." He whispered her name over and over and brushed her hair with his hand.

Aiyana's heart pounded with love. Derek cared for her as much as she for him. "I love you, Derek. I came here for a reason and I'm certain that reason was you."

Derek gently released her and walked across the room to his wooden chest. He opened the lid and picked up a folded piece of cloth and handed it to her. She widened her eyes. Could this be what she thought it was? Was it what she had fought and bartered for? It was all she had wanted these past couple of weeks and yet she wasn't sure if she wanted it now. She had lost the wager but Derek returned it regardless. Ironically, the comb had been close to her all along, only an arm's length away. It wasn't even under lock and key. She looked up at him and merely asked, "Why?"

"Aiyana, last night when I almost lost you I realized I couldn't just take what I want. I could not force you to do as I wish by bribery. And that was what I was doing for my own selfish purpose."

"Selfish? No way. It was for your brother."

"Because of my brother. I lost him and didn't want to lose you

159

too. I now know that even if I forced to you be with me it would be no guarantee that I would not lose you. That's how life works. There are no guarantees. So, Aiyana, I am asking you, please sail with me. Come of your own free will and be my bride. Love me forever as I will surely love you."

Aiyana felt dizzy, weak and strong all at the same time and it wasn't from the bump on her head. He had brought all her senses alive. Somehow they had been brought together and down to her very soul she knew they had been meant for each other.

Aiyana stepped forward into Derek's awaiting arms.

*a*iyana held Derek close, his breath caressed her cheek and pain clenched her heart. For as long as she could remember, Aiyana wanted nothing more than to compete in the Japanese kumite tournament. That was why since she arrived here, back in 1853, her primary goal was to get back her comb at all costs. But now she was here in Derek's arms and it was where she wanted to stay.

Derek was the true love of her life. He was the star meant to shine for her. She thought of their first evening together as geisha and danna. It was at the Tanabata Festival celebrating the legend of the weaver princess and shepherd. The gods had brought the lovers together but separated them again, by way of the Milky Way, because they neglected their duties. This ancient story could be hers and Derek's as well. Somehow the gods had brought her here, but, unlike the weaver princess, she would not allow herself to neglect her duties. Her duty was to complete what she had set out to do, in the present. Her lifelong passion and destiny awaited in the present time, this time was done and past.

Derek gently kissed Aiyana's cheek. By the solemn look on his face she figured he already knew her decision, without her even saying a word.

"Derek, this time I spent here with you, it rocked my world." He lifted his eyebrows and she continued to explain. "I feel like a different person than when I arrived. A part of me came alive, a part that I didn't know existed until now and for that I thank you, and for this." She lifted the wrapped comb in her hand. "Derek, trust me, if there was any other way I could be with you I'd go for it."

"I trust you, Aiyana. I've seen your integrity. It's one of the qualities that I love about you. That, and your vocabulary." His smile was subdued as he wiped her tears.

"I'm sorry, Derek, but I don't belong in this time. I have a life back home."

"I know. I've sensed it all along, even before I admitted it, and now it is time for me to stop fighting it."

She gave a crying laugh. "Pretty tough for a captain not to get his own way, huh?"

"Extremely."

"I love you, Derek," she whispered, feeling like a part of her was dying.

"Allow me," he said softly, his voice filled with emotion. He unwrapped the comb and dropped the handkerchief. She wanted to sear Derek's face into her mind forever. As long as she was alive, he would be with her.

He lifted the comb and smoothed back her hair. Tears streamed down her face. "Do not weep my love. Promise me something."

"Anything."

"Go and win your kumite." Derek secured the comb into her hair and time froze. A bright light shone into her eyes and Derek's face became translucent, almost ghost-like before it faded away. Her world spun around and she felt her body falling. She was slipping away. The last thing she remembered was calling out Derek's name. Then all at once, everything went black.

~

Aiyana lay on a cushion of warmth, aware of the gentle strokes of a cool cloth wiping her forehead. She smelled the familiar fragrance of iris and slowly opened her eyes.

"Mom?" She looked up at her mother who was sitting beside the bed. "Mom, you're here?" Aiyana looked around the room. There was a telephone on the bedside table, and a lantern emitting light from a bulb, not a flame. Her backpack was across the room on the floor.

"I'm back."

"Yes, thank goodness. How are you feeling dear?"

She looked at her mother's face, creased with worry. Aiyana had been on a journey that would be with her for a lifetime, a journey that felt real but logic dismissed as impossible. She was back in the present and ready to compete and fulfill her lifelong dream. Her heart pumped with excitement and anticipation and at the same time she felt a longing for a love that had just faded into the deep recesses of the past.

"Aiyana!"

She looked at her mother. "Oh, I'm fine. What day is it?"

"It's July 8th. I arrived about an hour ago and found you on the floor. The clerk helped me move you to the bed and he just went to call for a doctor."

It was only July 8th. In the past, weeks had transpired, but in the present, only one day had gone by. The seventh day of the seventh month. The one and only day when two stars were allowed to meet.

Aiyana sat up.

"No, Aiyana, lay down until the doctor gets here."

"I'm fine, Mom, really. But how's the bruise on my forehead?

Her mother stepped closer. "I don't see any bruise."

Aiyana palpated around her temple and felt no pain or any trace of a bump. It was as if she had never been injured. Her mouth dropped open. Had this all been a dream?

She felt shaky. "Mom, was there by any chance a comb in my hair, because it's not here now."

"Yes, as a matter of fact. It fell out of your hair when we moved you to the bed. It's beautiful, did you buy it here?"

She nodded. "Yes, I did." She swung her legs off the bed. "Where is it?"

"I wrapped it in tissue and zipped it into the front pocket of your knapsack."

"That's good, thanks." It was best left there. She had to focus on here and now. "Mom, when I left home, I didn't say good-bye, and you came anyway."

Her mother wrapped her arms around Aiyana. "My place is with my daughter. I realized when you left that I had made a dreadful mistake. So, I took the next available flight. I didn't even care about the cost, my credit card took care of it. I'm here where I belong."

Aiyana sighed. This must have been difficult for her mother, facing the memories of how her father had died, but this competition would be different—she would make certain of it. Aiyana squeezed her arms around her mother. "I love you so much. Thank you for being here."

"I can't very well miss my only daughter winning the kumite title, now can I?"

Aiyana beamed a smile of utter joy. She had her mother's support. The fever of competition pulsed through her veins. Now everything was up to her—well, almost.

CHAPTER 27

*A*iyana and her mother sat in the back seat of a taxi as it weaved through traffic. Within the highly urbanized setting Aiyana could pick out the occasional old building that she had previously seen, in another age. Or had she?

The taxi stopped abruptly and lurched Aiyana and her mother forward and then back. The driver looked in the rear-view mirror and blurted out, "Coliseum."

While her mother fiddled with the foreign currency, Aiyana stepped out of the vehicle, swung her gym bag over a shoulder and stared at the massive, domed building. The honking and noisy traffic faded into the background as her heart leaped and competitive excitement shook her stomach.

Her mother joined her. "I think I gave him too much of a tip. He's still bowing." She stopped and followed Aiyana's gaze. "Take a good look, honey. You're really here."

Aiyana nodded. She was really here and this all seemed surreal. She was finally living out what she had imagined so many times in her mind. But at this moment, while realizing her dream, she felt a sad, dull ache inside. She knew why but fought to put a name to it. To succeed, her whole being had to be here, in the present. Her focus mustn't wander.

"Ready, Aiyana?"

Aiyana smiled. "Absolutely."

They walked across the parking lot and joined a line at the entrance. Inside the front door stood two men dressed in red, ancient samurai uniforms with swords hanging by their sides. Aiyana jumped back and her mother looked at her with a questioning brow.

"Scary looking, aren't they?" her mother said.

"Very." If her mother only knew.

Inside the long foyer people crowded around vender tables selling karate items such as nunchuks, bows and mouth guards. They walked by a food concession stand and stopped at the registration desk.

"Hello, I'm Aiyana Amari, here to check in. Oh, and can you please leave a guest ticket for someone?"

"As you wish," the clerk said and handed several papers to Aiyana. The top sheet listed her fight times and the rings she would be in. Aiyana signed an accident waiver and then noticed her mother's worried expression before she paced away.

Aiyana signed. She had been so self-absorbed that she hadn't thought about how her mother was feeling. The last time her mother was here was on the tragic night many years ago. Still, the memories lingered.

"Hey, Mom," Aiyana caught up with her mother who had just wiped away a tear. "I have to go get changed now."

Her mother hugged her. "Good luck, honey. I'll be watching."

Aiyana spoke softly in her mother's ear. "I don't want you to worry. Things are different than when dad was here. We just have to believe things happen for reason and we can't be afraid of the future."

Her mother smoothed a hand along Aiyana's cheek. "My darling girl, when did you become so wise?"

Aiyana shrugged slightly, thinking back. Her time away, whether it had really happened or not, had changed her.

"Oh," her mother said, interrupting Aiyana's thoughts. She reached into her bag and handed Aiyana a bottle of Evian.

"Thanks, Mom. I love you." With a final glance behind and wave, Aiyana headed down the corridor to the change rooms. In the distance she heard echoes of cheering and applause. She dropped her bag and ran to look in the arena. The large floor space was divided into several rings, all of which had matches underway. The center ring was reserved for the championship fight.

The competitors wore gis of varying colors, each color unique to their club. Butterflies swarmed in Aiyana's belly.

I can do this.

She turned, retrieved her bag and went into the change room. Several competitors scattered along benches around the room. They were in various states of dress and exercise. Most of them simply glanced at Aiyana as she walked in but one Asian girl in a red gi with a gold dragon crest glared at Aiyana. Her competitor tightened her pony tail and threw punches in the air. Aiyana turned her back on the girl and changed into her black gi. She tied the belt in a perfect knot with equal length ends hanging. She stretched and performed a series of exercises and felt grounded and focused—even with the dragon girl squinting in her direction. Aiyana put on gloves, foot gear and held onto her mouth guard.

A man wearing a crisp white shirt and black pants holding a clipboard entered the room. "Aiyana Amari," he said.

"Here." Aiyana followed the official when suddenly the dragon girl blocked her way and eyed her up and down. This competitor was laying on the intimidation routine a little too thick and Aiyana laughed.

"Hey, save it for the ring," Aiyana said. "There are no judges here." She stepped around the girl and felt something hit her in the head. She looked back and saw a bottle cap rolling on the ground. Dragon girl then turned her back to Aiyana. Aiyana's pulse spiked and she forcefully exhaled. She wouldn't let this girl affect her.

She caught up with the official and he escorted her to the ring. Cheering and yelling from the crowd resonated in her ears and she glanced to the stands but couldn't find her mother. But, more importantly, she knew she wasn't alone. Her mother was here and Aiyana knew her father was watching as well, and in her heart, someone else.

She popped in her mouth guard and bowed before entering the ring. There she came face to face with her first competitor. The other girl was taller and heavier but Aiyana wasn't afraid or intimidated. Size and weight were not indicators of kumite skills. Aiyana's senses heightened and she zeroed in on her opponent. They bowed to each other and locked eyes the whole time. Aiyana stood ready, knees bent, fists up. When the referee gave the signal the match began. Immediately Aiyana attacked. Her punches felt electric in speed and power. Her opponent tried to score but her skills and speed didn't equal Aiyana's. In moments the referee raised Aiyana's arm and declared her the winner. Aiyana removed her mouth guard looked out into the crowd once again. This time she saw her mother waving and jumping. Aiyana smiled and waved back. She had completed her first hurdle.

She had only ten minutes before she was called for her second match. She refocused on the task at hand and after a gulp of water she stood, ready for the next fight.

She was victorious again, and again, moving toward the top of the pyramid. The next fight was the semi-final, if she won the one after would be for the championship. The thought of possible victory sent a rush of adrenaline through her.

She faced her next opponent. This girl was shorter than Aiyana, but stockier and her brown bangs hung down to her eyes. They stood there ready. The referee gave the signal and they started. They hopped on the balls of their feet. As usual, Aiyana lunged in with quick punches and successfully scored the first point. The other girl threw punches and kicks that were too short, missing their mark.

Aiyana moved and with a sidekick scored her second point. One more to go. She stood ready for the final round. Before the signal, her opponent lunged forward and kicked Aiyana square in the abdomen. A cheap shot. Aiyana slumped forward and dropped to her knees.

A whistle blew and a referee came over and asked if she was all right. Aiyana nodded as she struggled to pull air into her lungs. It felt like a cannon ball had rocketed into her stomach and it hurt to stand. The referee hadn't addressed her opponent, who should have been penalized but wasn't. Aiyana was shaken physically and now mentally. Improper ruling could have cost her the championship.

They prepared once again. Aiyana focused on her power-house counterpart and her goal. She had to block out the pain and anger. They circled each other, once, twice. In quick succession, Aiyana threw punches and a side kick. The official raised her arm and declared her the winner of the match.

Aiyana went to the side ring, wiped her face with a towel and sat on a folding chair. She almost started crying from joy and relief of making it to the championship fight. She shook inside and felt her focus scattering. Never in her life had she felt this kind of intense pressure. Years of training had led up to the next few minutes. She took a deep breath and had to get it together, now. Suddenly she felt hands on her shoulders and she turned.

"Mom." She got up and hugged her mother tightly. "Mom, you were right. I have always put too much emphasis on this. I got so far, but what if I lose?"

Her mother pulled back and held Aiyana's face. "Do not doubt yourself now. I was wrong. Sitting up there I was so proud of you and I know your father is too. Now, how's your stomach?"

"Better."

"When I saw your opponent do that cheap shot I wanted to do some punching and kicking of my own."

Aiyana laughed. "And I thought I inherited this all from dad."

The overhead speaker squealed. "Competitors, report to center ring."

"Aiyana, you know what to do honey. Win or lose—you're already a champion."

Aiyana put a fist to her heart then pointed to her mother.

"So are you."

a spotlight shone on the center ring. Aiyana stood at the periphery and stared at the canvas floor that through the years saw blood and tears, shed in the quest for the ultimate win. Cool air descended and a shiver ran through her. She glanced at the four judges stationed around the ring then out to the spectators. Not a seat was vacant. She took a deep breath and focused inward.

The two-minute warning gong sounded. Across from her she saw her opponent. Aiyana recognized the red gi and gold chest. Dragon girl. She was Aiyana's height but thicker and probably more muscular. Aiyana put on her protective gear and inserted her mouth guard. She did a few shoulder rolls and side head tilts before the referee told them to enter the ring. They walked to the center of the ring and kept their eyes locked on each other and bowed. They stood ready. This girl's black eyes squinted, trying to bore into Aiyana. But Aiyana wasn't fazed. She had a fight to finish.

The start signal was given and they immediately moved, hopping, circling. Aiyana advanced to perform a punch combination and gained the first point.

The girls set up again, face to face, and again they were signaled to begin. Almost immediately her opponent scored on her with a quick punch-kick combination. The score was one all.

They began again, bouncing and rotating around each other. Before Aiyana could strike, her opponent scored again with flash speed. Two-one.

For the first time today Aiyana was trailing. Dragon girl was a formidable opponent. She was quick as lightning. Aiyana's mind raced. This could be over very soon. Her opponent was beating her with the same offensive speed tactic that she herself used.

The referee gave them a minute to get a drink. Aiyana took a single gulp and wiped her mouth with her sleeve. She glanced out at the crowd but saw no familiar face. The audience was chanting and cheering so loudly that Aiyana wanted to cover her ears. Butterflies returned with a vengeance. She had trained so hard to get here and in minutes this would all be over. She was down points and there was a very real chance she wasn't going to win.

She had to stop her negative train of thought. Aiyana took a deep breath. *Everything happens for a reason.* She glanced at the crowd one more time and standing on the sideline was the kind woman from the souvenir shop. Aiyana waved at her and she bowed.

Suddenly she realized that this was more than a fight. In this moment she was trying to be all that she could be: physically, mentally and spiritually. She closed her eyes and freed her mind.

Derek.

Until now she had pushed memories of Derek aside and kept his kumite advice in the past. She had reverted to how she used to fight before she had met him. If she didn't change her tactics then she wouldn't have learned anything at all. It was time to trust her instincts, just as Derek had said. Instead of sticking to a specific routine she would do what he said and feel out where the fight was going. She breathed deeply. She took her spirit to another place, somewhere she had been before, somewhere she was warm and one with the universe.

The fight wasn't about winning or losing. Not anymore. It was about being the best she could be and trusting all that she was.

The warning gong sounded. She opened her eyes, now barely noticing the noise from the crowd.

Aiyana and her opponent stood ready, frozen until the signal was given. Aiyana's senses felt alive, every micro-fiber of her being was ready to react. And without thinking, only using her senses and reflexes, she evaded her opponent's attack and countered with her own. Two all.

The competitors backed up and stood ready for the final time. One more point and it would all be over. The start signal was given and they immediately moved about. Her opponent punched and kicked but Aiyana successfully evaded and blocked. Suddenly the girl charged forward and yelled before kicking Aiyana in the side of the knee. Aiyana saw sparks of white as pain exploded in her leg. She screamed and dropped to the ground. She panted while waiting for the pain to subside. But it wasn't. A couple of referees and medical personnel ran over to assess her injury. She stood but couldn't put weight on her leg. The two executives each took an arm and helped Aiyana to a chair and the medical officer put an ice pack on her knee. Searing pain throbbed and tightened like a blood pressure cup.

"Are you able to straighten your leg?"

She slowly moved her leg. "I think so. Ahh, here, take the ice. It burns." She gently massaged her knee. "Was there a penalty called?" she asked through clenched teeth.

"No. No penalty," the official said.

"What?!" Aiyana couldn't believe it wasn't called. She glanced to the other side of the ring. While smirking, dragon girl stared at her. The attack had been deliberate. The girl wanted to win by default.

"Aiyanasan, what do you wish to do?" the official said. "Continue or forfeit?"

Aiyana's body tensed and her pulse accelerated. She had come too far and trained too hard to allow someone unworthy to win. Aiyana glared at the dragon girl but spoke to the official. "I wish to continue."

Aiyana stood. Her knee ached but felt surprisingly strong. As she walked the pain intensified her focus and determination. The gong sounded and Aiyana limped into the starting position across from her opponent. Suddenly, the girl didn't seem so smug, and a crease lined her brow.

The signal was given and the match commenced. Aiyana didn't hop around in circles but merely pivoted—ready to deflect, ready to strike. Her opponent punched, Aiyana blocked. For a fraction of a second dragon girl's eyes looked down at Aiyana's knee. Aiyana shifted position and attacked with lightning punches and a final roundhouse kick. Aiyana propelled the girl onto her back and stood over her in a ready-to-punch pose. Dragon girl was at her mercy, taken down. Defeated.

Aiyana slowly stood, not taking her eyes off the girl. The official raised Aiyana's arm and declared her the winner. Her opponent scrambled up, stomped out of the ring and threw off her gloves. When she was out of sight Aiyana looked around and saw the crowd in the stands on their feet, applauding, cheering and chanting her name. The woman from the shop was gone. She waved and bowed to the four corners and then saw her mother whistling in the first row. Aiyana couldn't smile any wider.

A tenth degree black belt judge in an elaborate purple robe went to Aiyana. They bowed to each other and he handed her the championship belt bearing a gold crest with the image of Mount Fuji and the words, Meiji Kumite Champion. It was beautiful. Tears wet her eyes as she held the belt high over her head.

This is for you, Dad.

Aiyana was swarmed by the press's flashing cameras, video

cameras and microphones. She conducted interview after interview for newspapers and TV stations she'd never even heard of. Much later she and her mother exited the arena. Aiyana held her mother's hand as she limped outside. Before getting into the taxi she took a final look at the stadium. This was her biggest and final competition. Then she looked up at the night sky, sparkling with stars.

Thank you, Derek, where ever you are.

CHAPTER 29

The forward thrust of the plane pressed Aiyana back into her seat. Her mother couldn't get on the same flight as her so once again she flew alone, but this time didn't feel alone. She looked out the small oval window as buildings, roads and white-capped Mt. Fuji grew smaller and smaller. Soon all she saw was the cottony clouds that enshrouded the plane.

It wasn't long ago when she saw the same clouds on her way to Japan, everything was so uncertain then, her mind was full of anticipation and unanswered questions about her fate. But now, everything had unfolded and everything was revealed—more had happened than she could have ever imagined. So much more.

How would she ever know what had really happened to her? All logic told her time travel was impossible. But, was everything that happened logical? Could everything be explained rationally?

The flight attendant handed Aiyana a ginger ale and as she sipped she thought of the moment she had met Derek. Until now, she had forced away any thoughts of Derek—she had to. The competition had to take priority. She wouldn't have been able to focus properly while nursing a broken heart. But now, she could open a window and allow herself to remember all the magical and sensual times they spent together. She missed Derek terribly and the thought of never being able to see him again hurt her deeply inside. Unlike her knee injury, it was a pain nothing could ease.

Her journey back in time may have been a dream, coma or even a near-death experience—she would probably never know. Aiyana pulled out her knapsack from under her seat and set it on her lap. She looked down at the small zipper in front and thought of what it housed. She hadn't looked at or held the comb since Derek had put it in her hair. As strong as she was physically, she was afraid she wouldn't be able to handle the heartache of seeing it again. Physical pain she could endure, but emotional hurt wasn't as easy to contend with. But, now she was ready. Ready to hold onto the one tangible item that linked her to Derek.

Aiyana pulled open the zipper and reached inside the pocket. Her fingers found the comb and she pulled it out. She held the cool metal in her palm. It remained cool. Had she imagined it getting warm before? She turned it over and widened her eyes to try to believe what she was seeing.

The row of pearls used to have an empty crevice, but didn't anymore. The groove was filled with a perfect, iridescent pearl. Aiyana's lips trembled. Pearls occurring spontaneously in the wild were extremely rare, but Derek dove and found one for her.

The impossible had become possible. The unbelievable, believable. She had proof that what she lived was real—proof she had gone back in time.

Tears flowed down her cheeks. Somehow she had become the Weaver Princess and Derek was the Shepherd, allowed to meet for a short time. Like the stars in the sky, her love for him would last forever. Perhaps one day the gods would intervene once again. Meanwhile, she would wait for that day to find love again. Until then, she had much work to do, which was good. What better way to heal an aching heart than by distraction? She would update the gym and with her new title and publicity, memberships would increase. Finally people would come back to authentic martial arts and kumite.

Aiyana looked at the comb. Could it happen again? Whenever she wanted? She longed to see Derek again. She hesitated and then combed some hair back and then pinned it in. She froze and waited for signs of dizziness or blackness. She waited but nothing happened. Her heart sank. The cabin lights dimmed and she snuggled back in her chair. Her eyes drifted shut and she fell into a deep dreamless sleep. When the plane's wheels hit the runway she awoke. She was home.

Fellow passengers eagerly pulled down their overhead luggage and organized their items before filing out of the plane. Aiyana sat with her bag on her lap and waited. She was in no hurry. She touched her comb to make sure it was still in her hair. She sat until the last person walked by. A flight attendant came over and asked if she was all right. Aiyana nodded and tried to smile.

"I will be," she said and stood up. She slung her backpack over her shoulder and from the overhead bin she took down her duffel bag and championship belt. She stepped out of the plane and walked down the tunnel. When she entered the airport she saw two uniformed men. They were the pilots who had flown her home.

One of them was older with short salt and pepper hair and a pleasant face. He smiled at Aiyana and tipped his hat.

"Thank you for flying American," he said.

She smiled. "Thank you for bringing me home."

Then Aiyana glanced up at the taller one when he turned. She stood immobile but her heart thumped hard. The man's hair was short brown, not blond, but it was his green-brown eyes she'd seen before. And his expression reminded her of Derek. She shook her head. She had to be hallucinating.

"Nice trophy," he said in a smooth deep voice. "Did you win it?"

Her jaw dropped. It was as if Derek had asked her that question himself. She nodded. "I did."

He was polite and formal but showed no signs of recognizing her. She was missing Derek so much that she was trying to wish him back to her. She managed to utter a good-bye and walked away. She wasn't twenty feet away when she slowed her pace. Still, she wasn't ready to give up. She felt like she had to go back and see him. If she didn't do this she was sure she'd regret it for the rest of her days. When she turned around she noticed the older pilot was gone and the younger one bent over and picked up his satchel.

"Excuse me." Aiyana ran over.

The man looked at her and again his familiar eyes took her aback.

"Yes?" he said.

"I'm sorry, I was just wondering what your name is."

"It's Ryan. Ryan McPhee."

"Oh." Aiyana was instantly disappointed. "It was nice to meet you, Ryan McPhee." Her shoulders slumped and she turned to walk away again. She had been wrong. But now something made her stop, like an invisible arm prevented her from moving forward. When she turned, she noticed Captain McPhee hadn't moved, he had stayed where he was, looking at her. Then he started walking toward her. Aiyana held her breath.

"Are you missing anything?" he said.

"Not that I know of."

He held out his hand. "Is this yours?"

She looked down and saw her comb. Somehow it had fallen out of her hair. "Oh, yes it is. Funny, I hadn't realized it fell out. Thank you." She reached for the comb and her fingertips touched his palm. The warm light touch ignited her senses and she took a breath. "Umm, Captain, would you mind if I asked you one more question?"

He smiled and his dimples sent her heart racing. "Of course not."

"This may sound forward or weird, but I was wondering why you became a pilot?"

"That's not a strange question at all. I became a pilot because I have always been fascinated by aviation and the technology involved with it."

"I see," Aiyana said quietly. That wasn't the answer she had wanted to hear, but unexpectedly, he continued.

"But, the real reason I became a pilot was to have aviation skills. That way, nothing or no one would be too far from me. The world would be my port."

Aiyana choked up. That had been Derek's exact answer. Her heart raced wildly and she knew that somehow this was Derek. He had spanned the breeches of time to be with her. The gods had once again intervened and taken away the barrier of the Milky Way and allowed them to see each other once again, not for a day, but for a lifetime.

"And what do you think of this port?" she asked in a shaky voice.

"I like it here, what I have seen so far. May I carry that for you?" He gestured to her duffel bag.

"Oh, it's okay, I'll manage." She cringed inwardly. Must she always be so independent?

"Please allow me." He took it out of her hands. "And I would be honored if you would have dinner with me, maybe grab a burger, and perhaps teach me some kumite?"

Aiyana smiled at him, her heart overflowed with warmth and promise.

"Yes, Captain, I would love to."

ACKNOWLEDGMENTS

I'm grateful to my editor, Gail Martin, Laura Baumbach, and the whole team at Passion in Print for the first publication of this story.

Many thanks to Christine d'Abo for this beautiful new cover design and for playing the major role in this re-release. You rock!

Thank you to my awesome writing group—Magda Gold, Diane Kowalyshyn and Tim Simmons. I couldn't have done this without you.

Thank you to my family. Your love and support mean EVERYTHING.

ABOUT THE AUTHOR

Prior to writing, Judy was a professional figure skater and toured with the International Holiday on Ice Revue. After graduating from college she became a medical laboratory technologist and works in pathology. Her current focus is to create stories with interesting plots and characters she hopes readers will enjoy.

Judy loves spending time with her family in Hamilton, Ontario, Canada.

Visit Judy's Website!